DATE DUE

3-26-02			
Jan 3, 2005			

Absolute Beginners

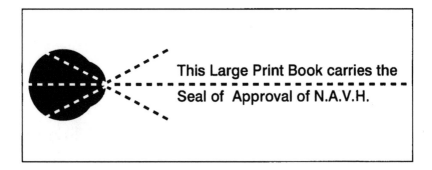

This Large Print Book carries the
Seal of Approval of N.A.V.H.

Absolute Beginners

COURTNEY RYAN

Thorndike Press • Thorndike, Maine

Published in Large Print by arrangement with
Sharon Jarvis & Co., Literary Agency

Thorndike Press Large Print® Romance Series.

The tree indicium is a trademark of Thorndike Press.

The text of this Large Print edition is unabridged.
Other aspects of the book may vary from the original edition.

Set in 16 pt. Plantin by Al Chase.

Printed in the United States on permanent paper.

Library of Congress Cataloging-in-Publication Data
Ryan, Courtney.
    Absolute beginners / Courtney Ryan.
      p.   cm.
    ISBN 0-7862-2489-4 (lg. print : hc : alk. paper)
    1. Women journalists — Wyoming — Fiction.
  2. Bodyguards — Fiction. 3. Wyoming — Fiction. 4. Large
type books. I. Title.
PS3568.Y274 A64 2000
813′.54—dc21   00-021592

Absolute
Beginners

CHAPTER

One

"The Monroe County jail is not a nice place for an innocent woman."

"Who says she's innocent?" Chris Hogan wedged the telephone receiver between his shoulder and chin and speared a juicy piece of tenderloin off his plate. "Maybe she's guilty as sin. Maybe the celebrated Jamie Cross has a thing for nasty movies. Have you ever thought of that, Murphy?"

"Give me a break. They were showing *Bimbos from Satan's Spa* when the police raided the theater. Does that really sound like the *Miami Tribune*'s Pulitzer Prize baby?"

"Don't ask me. I've only met baby once, remember? You introduced us when I came to pick up for lunch last week. The famous Ms. Cross working at her computer terminal, talking on the phone, and filling in an expense report, all at once. Other than her being a maniacal reporter, I didn't get a real good fix on her character. Although" — he paused to take a bite of asparagus — "I'd be willing to bet she has a bottle of Maalox in her desk drawer. All you maniacal reporters have ulcers."

"Trust me, Hogan. Jamie was checking out a lead for a story and just happened to be in the wrong place at the wrong time. Didn't your mommy ever tell you not to talk with your mouth full?"

"You did track me down at a restaurant," Chris replied, eyeing his date warily across the table. The lovely Estelle was beginning to pout. He passed her a basket of sourdough bread and shrugged helplessly. "I don't appreciate being telephoned in the middle of my dinner, Murphy. If I want to chew in your ear, I'll damn well chew. More wine, angel?"

"No thanks, lambikins," Murphy said.

"I was talking to Estelle." Chris could hear Estelle's heels tapping beneath the table. Tap-tap-tap — *tap-tap-tap*. . . . "Look, why don't you call a lawyer, Murphy? Don't you ever watch the television advertisements? Everyone knows you're supposed to call a lawyer for these delicate situations."

"Not if you know an ex-cop turned private investigator who can get the job done in half the time. As managing editor of the *Tribune*, I've learned the value of shortcuts. Just have a word with your old buddies at Monroe County. If I know you, you'll have

Jamie out of there before the ink on her fingertips is dry. What do you say?"

"We haven't had our dessert yet."

"Well, tell Esther an emergency has come up. She can stop at Dunkin' Donuts on the way home if she wants dessert."

"Her name is Estelle," Chris said softly. "And this one is going to cost you *plenty,* Murphy old pal."

"I realize that!" Murphy said cheerfully. "But you won't cost me nearly as much as a lawyer would."

The Monroe County jail was a terrible place for an innocent woman.

Jamie Cross sat on a hard wooden bench in a cold little cell and rubbed at the stubborn ink smudges on her fingertips. No doubt this was a clever trick of the law enforcement officials. Permanent ink, forever branding anyone with a criminal record. Jamie would have to wear gloves for the rest of her life. Who would have thought when she agreed to meet her informant in that blasted theater that it would end like this?

"Out damn spots," Jamie muttered. "I don't believe this. I've been thrown in the slammer. Tossed in the clink. A prisoner, a captive, a jailbird. I'll never see sunlight again." She glanced up at her cellmate, a

sullen-faced young woman sporting a startling mohawk. "You'll have to forgive me. I'm a writer."

"You're full of it," the woman snapped, vaulting to the top bunk in the cell.

So much for conversation. Jamie gave up on the ink smears and began chewing her nails. How long had it been since she had made that all-important save-me-if-you-can phone call? Three, four hours? Maybe it had been a mistake to call Mick Murphy. As her managing editor, he'd been on her case to ease up on the rather dangerous slant her column had taken lately. Perhaps he thought a few days in lockup would tame her crusading spirit. Jamie's investigative reporting had won her a Pulitzer Prize nomination, a weekly column in the *Miami Tribune*, and an impressive list of enemies. In the beginning, of course, Murphy had little to complain about. He was a logical and astute man who understood the mechanics of investigative journalism. A well-documented exposé inevitably resulted in an occasional lawsuit, a few nasty letters, and increased circulation. As long as his reporters weren't being shot at, Murphy was willing to take a bit of heat.

Lately, however, Murphy was afraid the heat was becoming an inferno. Jamie's latest target was a powerful Miami land developer with ties to organized crime. Jamie's articles alluding to Mr. Jon Miselli's involvement with the underworld had resulted in a flood of litigation, not to mention rumors of more serious retaliation against Jamie herself. Murphy claimed to be having nightmares about bullet-ridden reporters. His instinct told him it was time Jamie stopped playing the Lone Ranger, just long enough for things to cool down. He thought an article exposing miracle wrinkle creams would make for a nice change. It was an order, politely cloaked as a suggestion.

Twiddling her stained thumbs in her bleak cell, Jamie couldn't help but wonder if Murphy was making his point by taking his own sweet time in coming to her rescue. He had received the news that she had been meeting an informant when the theater was raided with ominous calm. Obviously he realized Jamie was continuing with the Miselli investigation. Jamie couldn't help but be a little nervous about that. Murphy was a patient man, but he did have his limits. Perhaps he thought a little quality time in the Monroe County jail would be just what his rebellious reporter needed.

"He wouldn't," Jamie said aloud. "He

couldn't. That would be so *petty*. He'll be here. Any minute now he'll be here."

The mohawk bobbed on the top bunk. "Well, goody for you. Now shut your face and let me get some sleep."

Jamie sighed, dropping her head in her hands. "Why couldn't they have put me in solitary?"

"Something wrong with the company?" her roomie snarled.

It had been a frustrating and humiliating night. Jamie was too tired to hold back. "Of course not. You're a delightful conversationalist. And your hair is lovely. Let's be best friends."

"How would you like your teeth shoved down —"

"Ladies, ladies." The trusty was peering through the bars, a heavy-set, gray-haired man with sorrowful, basset-hound eyes. "Is this any way to talk? Next thing you'll be spitting like a couple of wildcats and pulling out each other's hair. It's a good thing you're getting out of here, Ms. Cross. I think Stacey here would pretty well wipe the floor with you. She's one of our Saturday night regulars."

"I'm getting out?" Jamie jumped up from the bench, copper hair swinging in a bright arc. "I've been sprung?"

12

"Sprung?" a male voice drawled behind the trusty. "Three hours in the slammer and she's already picked up the lingo. What an ear."

"Meet your savior," the trusty said, stepping aside.

Jamie could only stare. Her savior was wearing a pale gray suit, white dress shirt, and paisley tie. The face was familiar, yet she couldn't recall a name. He was tall and slim, with longish honey-colored hair layered in thick, choppy waves. He had Baryshnikov eyes, heavy-lidded and intensely blue against the sun-kissed richness of his skin. Beautiful eyes, glittering with humor, curiosity, intelligence . . . every quality but innocence. Oh yes, she definitely remembered those eyes. But from where?

"You're bailing me out?" she asked.

"They're finishing the paperwork right now," he replied.

"That's very nice of you," Jamie said. Then, abruptly: "Besides being my savior . . . who are you?"

Chris smiled in spite of himself. This wasn't exactly the way he had pictured his evening ending, but the situation had its charms. Here was the illustrious Jamie Cross, that preoccupied bundle of frantic

13

energy he had met in the newsroom, staring at him from behind bars. The red-gold hair he had last seen in a tight French braid now framed her face and shoulders in a bright tangle. Her eyes were very wide and very green, and there was mascara smudged beneath her lower lashes. She was much shorter than he remembered, perhaps five-two or five-three. For some reason she had seemed taller sitting at a desk than she did standing in a jail cell. "You don't remember me. I'm crushed."

"I do remember you," Jamie said quickly. "At least . . . I remember your face. I'm very good with faces . . ."

"But not so hot with names, apparently." He studied her intently, his smile stretching. "You know," he said suddenly, "there's something about incarceration that kind of takes the wind out of your sails. Sitting there on your little bench you looked almost . . . needy. I barely recognized you."

"That makes us even," Jamie replied tightly. "Please don't think I'm being ungrateful, but why are you bailing me out of jail when you barely recognize me?"

"I see you have an enquiring mind," Chris said. With that lost-waif shadow in her eyes and that stubborn tilt to her chin, the feisty

14

jailbird was nearly irresistible. Nearly. Chris had to remind himself that he had retired from the hero business. "We'll talk upstairs. I'll go see about the paperwork. We'll have you . . . *sprung* . . . in no time. Meanwhile, shake hands and make up with Stacey so she doesn't wipe the floor with you."

Jamie's enquiring mind came up with the answer as they were walking down the front steps of the Monroe County jail.

"You're Murphy's friend," she said suddenly, stopping dead in her tracks. "Now I remember — I met you in the newsroom last week. Murphy said you used to be a cop, and now you're a private investigator." She studied him intently, a little frown etching her brow. "Funny. You don't look like a cop. As a matter of fact, you don't look like a PI, either. You're too . . . normal."

"Thank you," Chris said. "I think." He placed his hand at the small of her back and propelled her firmly forward. "Never stand still on the front steps of the county jail on Saturday night. You're likely to be trampled."

Jamie had to skip every third step to keep up with him. He had very long legs. "So I suppose Murphy called you and asked you to use your contacts to bail me out?"

"I'm cheaper than a lawyer . . . or so he thinks." A ghost of a smile flitted across his mouth. "Just wait until he gets my bill."

Jamie dodged a scowling young man in a soccer uniform charging up the steps. What an interesting place this was. How grateful she was to be leaving it. "It would be nice to have a name to go with the face," she said. "So I can bless you in my prayers from now on."

"Chris Hogan." He glanced down at the small oval head that came just even with his shoulder. The light from the street lamps seemed to ignore him completely, settling happily on the shimmering copper curtain of her hair. She had a tiny nose, barely visible beneath the tangled fluff of her heavy bangs. She wore tight black jeans and an oversized white sweatshirt that couldn't quite disguise the woman's figure beneath. He also noticed that one of her sneakers had come untied, with a white shoelace dragging on the ground. This was not the same frenetic whiz kid he had met in the *Tribune*'s newsroom. The old protective instincts twitched a little when he saw her rubbing her eyes in a childlike, weary gesture. He began to fear for his cool impartiality.

"Thank you, Chris Hogan," Jamie said.

"And I'm sorry I forgot your name the first time. I suppose I get a little . . . preoccupied when I'm working." This was a major understatement. Jamie had been known to stay awake thirty-six hours straight when working on a story. She often forgot to eat, missing two and three meals before her angry ulcer brought her back to earth. Yes indeed, she was the major contributor to the newsroom's manic energy bank — but there was no need for this man to know her guilty secrets. Already he suspected her of frequenting sleazy movie houses.

"Don't worry about it," Chris said. "I've been friends with Murphy a long time. I've learned to recognize the glassy-eyed trance of a journalist lost in his work." He stopped in the parking lot beside a beige Fiat convertible. "Here we are. It's not fancy, but it takes me where I want to go . . . when it doesn't break down."

Jamie looked down at the car, then up at Chris. "Private detectives don't drive Fiat Spiders with plastic hula dancers hanging from the rearview mirror."

"They don't?" Chris opened the door for her, from the inside. The handle was broken. "What do they drive, pray tell?"

"Black 1965 Corvette Stingrays," Jamie said promptly, settling into the worn sheepskin seat cover. "Or if they have a quirky sense of style, they drive a beat-up Chevrolet Impala and play classical tapes on the stereo."

"I don't have a tape deck," Chris said. "And the radio's broken. Sorry about that."

It was a cloudy night, with a sky full of faded, fuzzy stars. Jamie gave Chris directions to her apartment, half-expecting him to gun the little Fiat and run a few red lights. After all, it was nearly three in the morning, and the streets were empty. It was certainly what *she* would have done. Instead he drove at a steady, pleasantly mundane speed, braking for every stop sign, every traffic light, and one extremely slow-moving beagle.

"You could go around him," Jamie suggested, watching the dog plod through the yellow beam of the headlights.

"I could," Chris said, "but why? It's not like I've got a pressing engagement." He thought of Estelle and sighed.

"Do you always drive like this?"

He stared straight ahead, fingertips drumming an easy rhythm on the polished oak steering wheel. "Like what?"

"So . . . leisurely." A tactful word, Jamie thought, pleased. Far better than sluggish or snaillike.

The lady had a definite problem with relaxing. Cocking his head, Chris studied the restless movements of her hands in her lap. "Not always. If I have somewhere to go in a hurry, I hurry. If I don't, I don't. It took me a few years, but I finally learned to go with the flow. What about you? Are you always this nervous?"

"I'm not nervous," Jamie said, stung. "I'm perfectly relaxed."

"You're biting your nails, you're flicking my hula dancers, you're fiddling with the knobs of a radio that doesn't work. You start to wriggle in your seat every time we stop for a red light. And you want me to believe you're perfectly relaxed?"

"It doesn't really matter what you believe," Jamie retorted, "but this is about as relaxed as I ever get."

"I have a nasty feeling you're probably telling the truth," Chris murmured.

Conversation was sparse for the next few blocks. Jamie held her fingers stone-still in her lap. She refrained from wriggling. Then her eyes fell upon the heavy silver lock on the wood-paneled glove compartment.

"Is that where you keep it?" she asked. "In the glove compartment?"

Chris flicked a wary glance at the animated face beside him. "Keep what?"

"Your gun."

"Nope."

"You don't have a gun?"

He sighed. "I have a gun. Right now it's home in my top drawer snug and cozy with my Fruit of the Looms. Are you always this inquisitive?"

Jamie thought for a moment. "Yes. My mother called it healthy curiosity."

"Oh, I don't know how healthy it is," Chris said evenly. "I've read your column in the *Tribune*, and Murphy's told me about Jon Miselli. When you decide to make an enemy, you don't fool around, do you?"

"Everyone talks about Jon Miselli like he's the angel of death or something. No matter how many sticky pies he has his fingers in, he's still just a man. A nasty little man with a receding hairline and a potbelly and a walrus mustache."

Chris snorted. "If you believe that —"

"Turn here," Jamie interrupted. "My building's the third one down on the right."

Chris parked the Fiat between a Harley-Davidson and a BMW. It was an old neighborhood, in the transition stage between slum and condo. Half the buildings were freshly painted and repaired, with leafless baby trees edging the curb in undersized concrete planters. Everything else waited patiently in various stages of disrepair.

Jamie's building apparently had yet to attract the eye of an enterprising developer. It was a somber warehouse with tiny gray windows and a boarded-up loading dock. The only entrance appeared to be a weatherbeaten wooden door with faint lettering reading OFFICE.

Jamie couldn't help but smile. It was always interesting to bring someone home. Her company had such difficulty coming up with something pleasant to say about her humble abode. "Home, sweet home," she said.

Chris looked at the dreary building, then at Jamie Cross. Why was he surprised? Nothing about this woman was quite what he had expected. "You live in a warehouse," he said pleasantly.

"Actually I live above the warehouse. The entire top floor is mine."

"I imagine you didn't have to fight too many people for it."

"Well, there wasn't a waiting list, if that's what you mean." Jamie fumbled with the car door, staring at the handle in surprise as it came away in her hand. "Oh, dear. Look what I've done."

"It does that all the time," Chris said. "It's very temperamental, my little Fiat. Here, let me." He leaned across the seat, pushing and twisting the handle back into place. His shoulder grazed the curve of her breast and a muscle in his cheek tightened. "It'll just take me a minute," he said, as much to himself as to her.

Jamie took a deep breath. "No problem." The top of his head was brushing her cheek. His honey-brown hair was wind-tossed and cool against her skin. His thigh nudged hers, his right arm stretched along the back of her seat. The car was full of him.

She suddenly felt the need to talk. "Actually the old homestead isn't as bad as it looks," she said lightly. "I've spent the last two years fixing the place up. I had the hardwood floors refinished. I had a huge stained-glass skylight installed. On a sunny day the living room is a rainbow. Oh, and the mural — I have this friend who's an artist and he painted this fantastic mural on the bedroom —"

There was no warning. The air above them suddenly seemed to explode in a hurricane of light and sound. Splintered glass rained down on the street, sparkling on the hood of the Fiat like an early-morning frost. Tiny fireballs suddenly dotted the street, the sidewalk, the front steps of the warehouse. Burning things, Jamie thought stupidly, covering her ears with her palms to ease the painful reverberations. She looked into the gutter and recognized one of her own slippers. It was charred.

Chris yelled something at her, his eyes glittering, the fall of hair across his forehead suddenly matted with blood. She couldn't hear him — she could hear nothing but the sound of the explosion, over and over. She shook her head helplessly, still cupping her hands over her ears. The air was so hot, it was hard to breathe.

Chris had Jamie up and out of the convertible without her ever touching a door. A tiny cinder was burning on the sleeve of her shirt, and he put it out with his hand. Putting his arm around her, forcing her to stay low, he pulled her across the street where a crowd of wild-eyed neighbors was gathering on a miniature plot of grass. Most wore robes or nightgowns; one young man was clutching a flowered sheet around his middle and carrying a can of beer. They were all talking at once, their mouths moving up and down without sound. Like Jamie, Chris's ears echoed with a high-pitched, singsong noise.

They collapsed on the front steps of an old brownstone. Jamie was shivering. Chris put his arm around her, but he didn't think she knew he was there. She was staring straight ahead, watching the smoke curling from the third-story windows of the warehouse. The top floor, Chris realized numbly. Jamie's floor. Home, sweet home.

I had a huge stained-glass skylight installed. On a sunny day the living room is a rainbow . . .

Something deep within him stirred to life, a gentle emotion, a tenderness he had thought long dead. He took off his jacket and tucked it around her shoulders. Her head turned in slow motion, the water-brightness of her eyes meeting his. Her face was blank.

His hand found hers and held it tight.

CHAPTER

Two

Jamie didn't trust herself to feel anything. Not yet. Instead she watched the poor confused neighbors wander the streets in their nightclothes. She watched an elderly woman in a seersucker housecoat pick up a scarf from the gutter and stuff it in her pocket. Jamie's scarf.

Her hearing came and went, like a television set having temporary audio difficulties. She heard the young man in the flowered sheet blame the bombing on terrorists. His audience seemed to ignore his theory, possibly due to his attire.

Chris Hogan had sat with her on the steps of the brownstone until police cars and fire engines filled the streets with even more confusion. Then he went off to do whatever it was ex-cops did in these situations. Now and again she caught sight of him in the flashing red lights of the emergency vehicles. His once-white shirt was gray, and his tie had disappeared. Someone had put a gauze bandage stained with iodine over the cut on his forehead. There was absolutely no expression on his hard-boned face.

Granted, she didn't know the man well, but he was obviously a pro when it came to disguising his emotions.

One of the neighbors offered a stiff little how-terrible-call-if-you-need-anything speech. Jamie wondered with wry detachment if the woman realized she needed absolutely everything.

Absolutely everything . . .

She gave her statement to someone wearing a silver badge and a khaki baseball cap. Then she waited on the steps for another fifteen minutes before she realized she had nothing to wait for. Her apartment was gutted. Her car was still impounded in the police lot and would remain there until Monday morning. Her neighbors might offer sympathy, but they weren't likely to offer a temporary home. Jamie kept brutal hours at the newspaper and was never home long enough to have become acquainted with her neighbors.

In short, she was in limbo.

"No time to waste," Jamie murmured, getting stiffly to her feet. "If I don't know where I'm going, it could take me a long time to get there."

She walked slowly through the crowd to the poor little Fiat. The hood was dusted with glass and wood splinters. The windshield was cracked. The sheepskin seat covers were dotted with tiny black holes that looked like cigarette burns. Numbly, mechanically, she reached for the chamois in the back seat and carefully brushed the debris off the hood of the car. There. At least the paint wasn't damaged.

"Kind of looks the part now, don't you think?" Chris said behind her.

Jamie turned, the motion causing a vague sense of vertigo. Perhaps she was more tired than she realized. "What looks the part?"

"The Fiat. With those battle scars, any private eye would be proud to drive it." He paused, studying the shadows beneath her eyes. He felt so damn helpless. "You look like hell." *That's the ticket, Hogan. She's bound to feel better now.*

She managed a pale smile. "You know how it is. Having your apartment bombed kind of takes the wind out of your sails. Besides, you aren't so pretty yourself. That bandage on your forehead looks pretty scary."

"A paramedic's job is to apply scary bandages. Underneath is nothing but a scratch."

"That's what all the macho private eyes say. 'Just a scratch, ma'am.' "

"You're an expert on private investigators?"

"I watch television." Jamie shook the chamois out and leaned over the car to drop it in the back seat. When she straightened she felt a wave of heat wash over her, making her feel lightheaded and dizzy. She took a deep breath of the smoky air but couldn't find any oxygen. The ringing in her ears was suddenly back.

Chris watched the color drain from her face. He moved quickly, catching her the instant her legs gave way. Her head lolled weakly against his chest, her hands clung to his shoulders. "I've got you," he said soothingly. "It's all right, I've got you."

"I'm just fine," she mumbled against his shirt. She tried to push away from him, but either she was still disoriented or his grip was stronger than she thought. "I was just a little dizzy for a minute. You can let me go, really."

"You sure you're all right?" He didn't sound convinced.

"Sure. Of course." She took another deep breath, focusing on the button of his shirt. Yes. The world had stopped spinning.

He released her slowly, staying quite close in case she decided to continue the fall he'd prevented. She looked like a gentle breeze would send her toppling. "Don't lock your knees like that," he said abruptly. "Just relax."

"Yes, sir." Her voice was hoarse from the heat and smoke.

They looked at each other for a long moment. Jamie's face was pinched and frozen. Chris smiled a sweet, sad smile and gently brushed clinging strands of hair from her cold cheek. "So where do we go from here?" he said quietly.

Her lips felt so dry, she had to moisten them just to talk. "There's no sense in my staying here. They won't let me back in the apartment to try and salvage anything until the bomb squad is through with their investigation. I thought I'd find a motel and try to get some sleep. I'll face all this in the morning."

"It is morning," he reminded her. "The sun will be up in a couple of hours."

"Then I'll face it at noon. I can't think now." Her eyes looked bruised in her pale face. "I really don't want to think now."

"I understand," he said softly. Absorbing the weary tension in her delicately shadowed face, he experienced an uncomfortable surge of emotion. Like Jamie, he decided not to think about it now. "Everything's going to be all right, Jamie. As a matter of fact, I know a nice safe place for you to get some rest."

Jamie leaned her head back against the seat and slept as they drove. At least, it seemed that she slept. The car's gentle vibration underscored the fragments of dreams in her mind. When she opened her eyes again, the Fiat's engine was silent, and the only sound in the world was . . .

"Crickets," she said, disoriented from fatigue.

Chris was opening her door, helping her from the car. "What about crickets?" he asked kindly.

"I hear them," she said. "I hear crickets. Where are we?"

"This is where I live," he replied, in that same tone. "We're in Santa Clara, near the beach, and this is my house. It has two bedrooms and two bathrooms and a nice tile roof. Oh, and I have orange trees. Can you smell them?"

Jamie nodded. She could smell the orange trees. She could also see the small Spanish-style house fuzzy yellow porch light. Chris Hogan's house. "I can't stay here with you," she said.

"No?" He began walking up the gravel drive, taking her with him despite her shallow resistance. "Why not?"

"I hardly" — she stifled a yawn — "know you."

"We were nearly blown up together. I bailed you out of jail. Of course we know each other."

"Chris, I don't think —"

"I realize that," he said, "but you're very tired and it's understandable. The facts are, you need a bed and I happen to have an extra one. Also, there's the matter of the little explosion tonight. Someone tried to send you nighty-night permanently. I think we would both sleep better if you stayed here where I can keep an eye on you. Now, are you going to give me any idiotic arguments, or are you going to be logical and rational?"

Did she have any arguments? Jamie wondered. No, she was too tired to argue. "That was a charming invitation. I couldn't refuse it. I don't have the energy to refuse it."

"I'm so glad," Chris said, unlocking the front door. "Because I don't have the energy to talk you into it. After you, Ms. Cross."

Jamie's strained eyes saw Chris's house through a gray veil of exhaustion. Her stuporous brain barely registered the smooth terra-cotta tiles in the entry hall, the soft beiges and blues in the living room. As they moved down a shadowy hallway, Chris's low-pitched voice penetrated to her consciousness.

". . . bedroom's right here and there's an adjoining bath. Oh, you'll need something to wear. Hold on a minute, I'll be right back."

He went into the bedroom across the hall. Jamie looked around for something to hold on to as he had suggested, but there was nothing. She leaned against the wall for support.

He returned in thirty seconds carrying a soft velour robe that he pushed into her hands. "Here. It'll drown you, but it's all I've got. I never wear pajamas to bed, so — well, never mind. Is there anything else you need?"

"No, I'm fine. Thank you." It was all she could do to form the words.

"Pull the drapes so the sun doesn't wake you."

"Thank you."

A suppressed smile flirted with the corners of his lips, even as the concern darkened his eyes. "You said that already. You're really out on your feet, aren't you?" He opened the bedroom door and pushed her gently through it. "Go to sleep, Jamie.

You've had all you can handle for one night."

She turned, staring at him unblinkingly. In the darkness, her glittering green eyes seemed to take up half her face. "I'm going to be fine," she whispered. "I'm very strong."

She looked so small and battered, yet instinctively he knew she was telling the truth. Gently he said, "I know."

He closed the bedroom door between them. Jamie looked at the bed, then sighed and stripped off her clothes with heavy, aching limbs. She couldn't possibly lie down covered with soot and grime. He'd never get the sheets clean again.

She sat down in the shower. She didn't have the energy to stand, and the stall was too small to lie down in. Then she wrapped herself in his robe and tumbled into bed, dripping hair and all.

Despite her exhaustion, she slept fitfully. Her dreams were an unfriendly mosaic, full of scorching fires and deafening explosions that went on and on, like fireworks on the Fourth of July. She roused herself to half-consciousness several times, trying to throw off the visions that haunted her. Had she been able to summon the strength, she would have spent the night sitting upright in a chair to escape those dreams. But fatigue had left her helpless, and sleep was a damnable necessity.

Awareness finally came with the hot sparkle of sunlight on her lashes. She opened her eyes to a room full of warmth and light, an unfamiliar room with white wicker furniture and a wall of floor-to-ceiling windows. Her hazy, drifting gaze fell on the open-weave curtains on either side of the windows. She'd forgotten to close them. Thank heaven. She was more than happy to leave her restless dreams in never-never land.

Her clothes had spent the last few hours in it heap on the floor. Not only did they smell like a bonfire, but they were wrinkled beyond recognition. Jamie took them into the bath and draped them over the shower door, then ran the hot water long enough to fill the room with clouds of steam. It was the next best thing to a steam iron — or so the Women's Editor of the *Tribune* had told her.

Her stomach was making horrible, threatening noises. Jamie could smell the heavenly aroma of coffee brewing beyond the bedroom door, beckoning her. She hesitated, wondering how bold she dared to be. Chris's voluminous robe was decent enough, certainly. She'd worn ski suits that were more revealing. The problem was the poor creature inside the robe. The mirror above the dresser was brutal. Jamie's hair was a frightening snarl, still damp in the back where she had slept on it. Her usually vibrant complexion was almost ghostlike, emphasizing the light scattering of freckles across her nose. Jamie hated those freckles.

On the other hand, she hadn't eaten since . . . when? Yesterday morning? Her ulcer was usually quite tame, but the strain of the past twenty-four hours had taken its toll. The hot rumbling in her stomach demanded food. Now.

She followed her nose down the hall, through the living room and into the obscenely bright kitchen. The floor was blue and white tile, the cabinets made of natural oak and finished with a clear varnish. Other than a bubbling coffee machine, the countertops were completely free of knickknacks and small appliances. Obviously a private investigator had more important things to do than putter around a kitchen.

And speaking of which, the man himself was seated on a bar stool with his back to the door, holding a portable phone to his ear with one hand and trying to spread butter on a piece of toast with the other. He was wearing soft blue jeans and a white T-shirt that was one cup of bleach away from being transparent. His feet were bare and from the back his hair looked every bit as tangled as Jamie's. Had he fallen into bed with wet hair, too?

Jamie remained quiet so as not to interrupt. She couldn't help overhearing.

"I realize it's the only option," Chris said, his knife chasing the toast across the slippery Formica counter. "But I still don't understand why I have to handle it. There has to be someone else who . . . no, it's not the money. I couldn't care less about the . . ." Silence. "That much? Are you kidding me? No, of course it doesn't make any difference. I'm just not — oh, hell. All right, I'll do it." Another silence, this time stretching to two or three minutes. "I understand. I'll take care of everything on this end. I'll be in touch."

He replaced the phone on the counter, the set of his broad shoulders suggesting he wasn't too pleased with the way the conversation had gone. He stabbed his toast with the butter knife, and Jamie jumped. The bar stool spun a quick half-circle.

"I'm sorry," she said. "I came begging for coffee. I didn't mean to eavesdrop."

"That's all right." Judging by the detached curiosity in her tone, Chris assumed she had happened in on the tail end of his phone call. Her attitude would have been dramatically different had she heard the entire conversation. "It was just business," he added nonchalantly. "So . . . how did you sleep?"

Jamie gave him a sleepy smile. "Pretty well, considering the explosions going off in the back bedroom."

His eyes sparkled beneath heavy lids. His scary bandage was gone, replaced by a flesh-colored Band-Aid. "I know what you mean. Every time I fell asleep, somebody set a bomb off under my bed."

"You give a mean slumber party," Jamie said. She was fascinated by his T-shirt. On the front was a slightly faded picture of a Saint Bernard, with the words BAD, BAD, BAD DOG lettered beneath. She couldn't help laughing. "Nice shirt, Marlowe. I used to have a Saint Bernard. 'Bad, bad, *bad* dog' was my mother's favorite expression for him."

"It's nice to see you laugh," Chris said softly. Her dark-lashed eyes were amazing, brilliant and warm and beguiling. The haunted shadows beneath those smiling eyes added a poignancy that rippled through his senses. Here it was again, he thought, that disturbing sensation called feeling. If he didn't watch himself, it was going to become a habit. Abruptly he got up from the bar stool, reaching into a cupboard for a coffee mug. "How do you like it? Cream, sugar?"

"Black will be fine," Jamie said quietly. She had sensed his withdrawal, though she didn't understand it. Perhaps she had overstayed her welcome. Chris had gone far above and beyond the call of duty as it was. "Have you any idea what time it is?"

Chris glanced at the watch on his wrist. "Nearly noon."

No wonder he was feeling restless. Jamie had no idea it was so late. He'd probably been hanging around the house for hours, waiting for her to wake up so he could go off and do . . . whatever it was private investigators did on weekends. She gulped the coffee he gave her, scalding her tongue. "I really have to go," she said. "I didn't mean to impose on you like this. Besides, I need to get down to the newspaper."

"It's Sunday."

"There's no such thing as Sunday when you work on a paper. I have a deadline staring me in the face. I have to get to work on it. Everyone's going to be wondering where I am."

"Your house was blown up last night," Chris said slowly, "and you're worried about getting to the office?"

Jamie shrugged. Not looking at him, she said lightly, "At the moment it's the only place I have to go."

Chris studied the shimmer of red-gold hair that curtained her face. "It's remarkable, isn't it?"

"What is?"

"The damage a nasty little man with a potbelly and a walrus mustache can cause."

She looked up then, and for a moment her wide green eyes were unguarded. Vulnerable. Then the brave little mask slipped back in place. "Miselli? You don't know that."

Chris held her gaze. "We both know that."

Jamie put the coffee mug down. "The police aren't going to find a shred of evidence linking Jon Miselli to that explosion."

"Oh, I'm sure they won't," Chris agreed dryly. "A man like Miselli specializes in clean hands. That doesn't change the facts."

Jamie busied herself brushing the toast crumbs on the counter into a neat little pile. "You seem to know quite a bit about the man."

"Don't forget, I was a cop for eleven years. Miselli may have clean hands, but his reputation is lousy. Unfortunately, you can't convict someone of a bad reputation." Chris moved closer, lifting her chin in the crook of his finger, gently forcing her to meet his gaze. "And as long as Miselli is hale and hearty and living in Miami, you're going to have yourself a hell of a kinked neck."

"Why?" Jamie whispered. She didn't know why she was whispering. It had something to do with his nearness, something to do with the shadowed intensity of his eyes. He was dead serious.

"From looking over your shoulder," he said simply.

She stared at him for a moment, catching her lower lip thoughtfully between her teeth. She could have told him that if he was trying to frighten her it wasn't necessary. She was already frightened. She could have told him that she hadn't slept well for weeks, that she felt isolated in her battles. But that would mean letting her guard down, giving Chris Hogan a glimpse into her vulnerable soul. That wasn't her way. "I should get dressed," she said quietly. She stepped back, away from his touch, away from the temptation to confide in him. "Would you mind if I used your phone to call a cab?"

"There's no need. If you want to go in to work, I'll drive you."

"No." The word came out more abruptly than she had intended. She took a deep breath, then said carefully, "No, thank you. I couldn't possibly impose on you again. As it is, I don't know how I'll ever thank you for everything you've done."

"You could pay me a large amount of money," Chris said, poker-faced.

Jamie blinked. "You want . . . well, I didn't . . . yes, of course . . ." She paused for air, shaking the hair away from her face. Then, a bit apprehensively, "Just how much do you think —"

"Idiot." Grinning, he nearly succumbed to the compulsion to pull her into his arms and kiss away that adorable confusion. Instead he contented himself with running the back of his fingers lightly down the soft heat of her check. "I don't want your money."

"I insist on paying for the damage to your car."

"Why don't you get dressed," he suggested sweetly, "before I decide to spank you? I'll telephone for a cab, Miss Independence."

Jamie paused in the doorway, facing him. "Macho soul that you are," she said solemnly, "this may come as a severe blow,

41

but . . . you're actually a very sweet man."

It wasn't until he had heard her bedroom door close that he said, "I wonder if you'll think so in an hour or two?"

Mick Murphy's office was a mess. There were several dirty coffee cups scattered here and there, a half-eaten danish on the bookshelves, an explosion of papers littering the desk and floor. Jedediah the hamster ran happily on his exercise wheel in the metal cage on top of the filing cabinet, filling the room with his own unique fragrance. All was well at the *Miami Tribune*.

Jamie slumped down in the chair opposite Mick's desk, cradling her purse in her arms. The imitation leather bag was the only personal possession she had left. It had become quite precious. "Time to clean out Jedediah's cage," she said by way of greeting.

Mick Murphy eyed his star columnist. "You're rather aromatic yourself. Been roasting marshmallows round the old campfire, Jamie?"

Jamie smiled tiredly. "Something like that." Murphy was a serene and imperturbable man in a profession that bred nervous breakdowns and bleeding ulcers. He was forty-four years old, with keen brown eyes and a startling, shaggy mane of black and silver hair. Jamie had always enjoyed Murphy's dry wit and easy-going personality. When he was city editor and Jamie was just another young neurotic in the newsroom, they had often worked the night through, munching on peanut-butter cups and pretzels while Murphy instructed her in the fine art of investigative journalism. At the time, Jamie had been desperately in love with a young attorney from the DA's office, a passionate, all-consuming affair that only the young and unscarred have the courage to begin . . . and end. True to his nature, Murphy had stood quietly by while she made every mistake in the book, then offered her a dry handkerchief and enough extra work to keep her too busy to think. The sympathetic lack of sympathy had been just what she needed. Then and now, Murphy's instincts were faultless.

"Something like that," Murphy repeated slowly, as if the words merited closer consideration. "I suppose that's your way of telling me your apartment was blown to smithereens early this morning."

Jamie had been afraid of this. It was so difficult to hide anything from a man who had twenty-four hour access to the police report. "I was going to tell you," she said. "I

43

was working up to it."

"Oh? Well, in that case" — Murphy leaned back in his chair and folded his arms across his chest — "please proceed. I'm all ears."

As briefly as possible, Jamie filled him in on the past twelve hours. She avoided mentioning Miselli's name completely, for all the good it did her.

"Miselli," Murphy said when she finished. "You know it and I know it, so let's not waste time kidding ourselves. The man has finally made good on his threats. I guarantee you he won't be pleased when he finds out you weren't tucked into bed when his little surprise package went boom. After all, he waited until three in the morning when all good little girls are supposed to be in bed. And then you had to get yourself arrested and ruin everything."

Jamie smiled sweetly. "I promise you I'll apologize to him in my next column."

"Such a funny girl," Murphy snapped. In a flash he was up and out of his chair, pacing the office with his hands shoved deep in his pockets. "I've always enjoyed your sense of humor. I'm going to miss it when you're gone. But I promise you, we'll run one heck of an obituary on you, kid. I'll write it up myself."

44

Jamie opened her eyes wide in mock confusion. "Gosh, Murphy, are you trying to tell me something?"

"Yeah, I'm trying to tell you something!" He stopped dead in his tracks in front of Jedediah's cage. His back was to Jamie, rigid and uncompromising. "I'm telling you good-bye."

Jamie was confused. Murphy seldom raised his voice or lost his temper, and today he was doing both. "Either you're firing me," she said slowly, "or you really don't expect me to live through the day. So which one is it, Murphy?"

"I'd fire you in a heartbeat if I thought it would keep you safe." Murphy turned around and Jamie felt the full force of his brilliant, burning gaze. "Unfortunately, Mr. Miselli doesn't care if you're employed or unemployed. You've made things very hot for him in Miami. I think that nice little bomb was just his unique way of returning the favor."

"So I'll back off for a while," she said. "I'll do a column for the food page or something. I'll give things a chance to cool down. I'll be very careful."

"You don't understand." Murphy returned to his worn leather chair, folding his big hands into a tight knot on the desk. "I

45

said I was telling you good-bye and that's just what I'm doing. You're going on assignment."

"On assignment?" Jamie gave a short, disbelieving laugh. "You've got to be kidding. I can't go on assignment. My home was just demolished. I have no clothes, I have no suitcases, I have no toothbrush. I haven't even contacted my insurance company yet. I have a few things to take care of, Murphy."

"I know," Murphy said tonelessly. "And it's all going to have to wait. You're going to Wyoming."

"I'm going *where?*"

"Wyoming. It's a great place. I visited there once about twenty years ago. Lots of birds and trees and things. You'll love it."

"You're putting me on," Jamie said slowly. "Right?"

Murphy held her gaze. "I'm keeping you alive. My sources tell me it's only a matter of time before the police move in on Miselli. Till then, you can enjoy the peace and quiet of Clearwater, Wyoming."

"I don't like peace," Jamie said. "I don't like quiet. I like concrete and smog and traffic jams. You *know* me, Murphy. I couldn't possibly survive west of the Mississippi."

"You have that backward, sweet. You can't possibly survive *east* of the Mississippi."

Jamie closed her eyes briefly. "I don't feel well, Murphy."

"A nice plane trip will perk you up."

"Why Clearwater? I don't know anyone in Clearwater. I don't know anyone in Wyoming."

"I do," Murphy said firmly. "My old college roommate has a summer home there which he has graciously offered for our use. It has all the amenities, right down to indoor plumbing. It's the perfect place for you to work on that novel you've always wanted to write."

"I never wanted to write a novel!"

"Nonsense. Everyone wants to write a novel." Murphy pulled a fat envelope out of his desk drawer and tossed it into her lap. "There you go. Two plane tickets, a bundle of cash, and detailed directions to the house. Your flight leaves at six tonight. You have just enough time to buy yourself a few things before you go. Put everything on your expense account."

"Murphy, I can't believe you really expect me to —" She paused, frowning. "Two plane tickets? Why two?"

"Well, what did you expect?" Murphy's expression softened slightly, his mouth tilting at the corners with a smile. "I wouldn't trust you to get on the damn plane. I've hired someone to look after you."

It took a moment for that to sink in. Then, with soft anger: "A bodyguard or a babysitter?"

Wisely, Murphy chose to ignore her question. "He's waiting down in the lobby now. He'll take you shopping —"

"Oh, wonderful."

"— then straight to the plane."

"And I'm supposed to live with this strange person for heaven knows how long in Clearwater, Wyoming?" Her thoughts were startled and jumping. "This arrangement is supposed to make me feel safe?"

"I can see I haven't explained myself very well. You don't need to *live* with him. He's simply going to escort you to Clearwater and see you safely settled in. He's an expert of sorts when it comes to security. After that, he'll be winging his way home. You should be perfectly safe, since there are only three of us who will know your whereabouts."

"I'm going to Wyoming with Dirty Harry," Jamie said dully.

"Think of it as a well-deserved vacation," Murphy offered grandly. "And by the way, your escort isn't really a stranger. As a matter of fact, the two of you have become quite close recently."

Jamie had just spent most of the night at the county jail. She had become acquainted with a number of people who specialized in security, none of them particularly friendly. Quite truthfully she said, "I'm afraid to guess."

"Then I'll give you a hint. You woke up wearing his robe this morning."

CHAPTER

Three

The employees of the *Tribune* knew Jamie Cross as a talented, unaffected woman with a breezy personal style. Her makeup was always applied with a deft hand, just enough to camouflage her freckles and emphasize her lovely deep-green eyes. Her clothes were always on the sporty side, casual and attractive. And clean.

The receptionist in the lobby barely recognized the young woman emerging from the elevator. Breezy was one thing — bedraggled was another. Jamie's clothes appeared to be covered with soot, as if she'd spent the morning cleaning chimneys. She wore absolutely no makeup. She had freckles on her nose and murder in her eyes.

Jamie was oblivious to the startled glances she was receiving. He was here somewhere, that conniving, blue-eyed Judas. She scanned the crowded lobby until she spotted him, her eyes locking with his over the shifting bodies and bobbing heads. She smoldered. Chris Hogan smiled.

They met in the center of the lobby where a miniature fountain gurgled over hundreds

50

of rusting coins. Pennies mostly, Chris noted. These journalists were a tight-fisted lot.

"You could have told me this morning," she said, her eyes glittering dangerously.

Chris looked startled. "The hell I could. Murphy made the decision. It was up to him to give you the happy news."

"You sound like you were afraid I'd break a coffee cup over your head or something. I'm a sane and rational adult, in case you hadn't noticed."

"You forgot volatile," Chris murmured.

Jamie closed her eyes briefly. Her ulcer gave a hot little twinge, reminding her it had been an extraordinarily stressful weekend, and she had yet to eat a decent meal. Food first, she decided. She would face the prospect of Clearwater, Wyoming, after she had something in her stomach. Quite calmly — thereby proving she was *not* volatile — she said, "I would like a bowl of clam chowder."

Chris's eyes were very bright in his sun-browned face. "Immediately?"

"Yes." Her expression dared him to argue with her.

Chris surrendered with a smile, feeling that internal tenderness nag at him again. "Yes, ma'am. Whatever you say, ma'am."

Jamie stared at him, all too conscious of the way his honey-colored hair drifted around his forehead beneath the fluorescent lights. Soft and shining, a halo for her reluctant white knight. His lean hips were molded in soft denim; a pale yellow shirt sculpted his torso. If he carried a gun, she had absolutely no idea where it might be.

"I heard you on the phone with Murphy this morning," she said abruptly. "You didn't want this job." There. It was out, the memory that was irritating her like a splinter beneath her skin.

There was only the slightest tightening of his lips to tell her she had struck a nerve. He looked at her for a long moment, the half-playful light in his eyes fading slowly. He swallowed once, hard. "I just want the best for you," he said tonelessly. "That's all."

Curiosity mingled with the impatience in Jamie's gaze. "Obviously Murphy thinks you're the best."

"Poor Murphy's been in the newspaper business too long," Chris said briskly. It was time to change the subject. For some reason which he didn't care to examine too closely, he'd agreed to take responsibility for Jamie's safety. He'd allowed Murphy to think that the money had tempted him. He'd even tried to convince himself he'd taken the job on behalf of his anemic bank account. Inwardly, he knew better. He might not trust himself any longer — but neither did be trust anyone else to look after Jamie Cross. In other words, he was caught between a rock and a diminutive redhead.

And said redhead's stomach was growling loud enough to be heard in Clearwater, Wyoming. "Clam chowder?" he asked.

Jamie sighed. "Please. I know a wonderful restaurant just around the corner."

On impulse, Chris flipped a coin into the fountain as they left. A silver dollar, as a matter of fact. *A hundred wishes on credit,* Chris thought. Not bad idea, all things considered.

Shopping with a bodyguard was difficult, particularly in the lingerie department.

"This is going to take a while," Jamie said pointedly. "I need slips and nightgowns and . . . everything. If you'd like to go sit down somewhere . . ."

"We don't have a while," Chris replied. He was looking at a black negligee on a red-headed mannequin. Yes, on Jamie that would be stunning. "It's now ten minutes to five. The plane leaves at six. You've got twenty minutes."

"I can't possibly buy everything I need in twenty minutes!"

"I'd give it a good try if I were you," he

advised dryly. "I'm really not sure what the stores in Clearwater have to offer." He thought for a moment. "Flannel shirts, maybe."

"This is impossible. I need shoes, makeup, lingerie."

"You're the one who had three bowls of clam chowder and two pieces of pie. What size are you? Eight, ten?"

She glared at him. *"Six."*

"You take care of the makeup and lingerie and I'll pick out some clothes."

"If you think I'm going to trust you to —"

"You've got eighteen minutes," Chris said calmly, "and counting. Would you really rather shop in Clearwater?"

Jamie took a deep, unsatisfying breath. If there was mercy anywhere in this situation, she certainly couldn't find it. "Nothing pink," she said finally. "It clashes with my hair. And no ruffles. Jeans will be fine. Jeans and T-shirts." How difficult could it be to pick out a nice pair of 501s?

Chris smiled broadly. "Not to worry. I have excellent taste."

They boarded the plane with three minutes to spare. Jamie's carry-on luggage included a makeup case and a large leather shoulder bag. She had no idea what was in the shoulder bag. It was rather heavy and made strange clinking noises when she walked. Chris had been carrying it along with a brand-new suitcase at the end of his eighteen-minute shopping spree.

The takeoff was rather bumpy, thanks to strong crosswinds blowing in from the sea. Considering the way her luck had been running, Jamie was pleasantly surprised they didn't lose an engine and crash-land in Biscayne Bay.

The moment the seat-belt light went off, Chris stood and fished the shoulder bag out of the overhead compartment. "Here," he said cheerfully, dropping the bag in Jamie's lap. "I packed a change of clothes for you. It's a terrific outfit, you're going to love it. And wrinkle-proof, or so the saleslady told me."

Jamie was touched. She had been longing to change into clean clothes; she simply did not have any clean clothes to change into. She was touched . . . and apprehensive. "This outfit . . . you picked it out yourself?"

Chris nodded.

"Jeans?" she said hopefully.

"Oh, I bought you a couple of pairs of jeans," he said nonchalantly. "They're packed in the big suitcase with everything else. I thought you'd want something more comfortable for the plane trip."

There was something in his eyes, something so guileless and helpful, Jamie was instantly on guard. That Boy Scout expression was new to her. She would have been more comfortable with his sleepy-eyed cynicism.

He waited in the aisle, stubbornly blocking the drink cart the stewardess was wheeling by. Jamie sighed, pulling her makeup bag from beneath her seat. If she was not going to change, she may as well make use of her new cosmetics. "This was very thoughtful of you," she said as she slipped past him. Her smile was doubtful.

"The restroom's that way," Chris offered, gesturing to the rear of the plane.

Fifteen minutes later she was plotting Chris Hogan's murder. When they flew over the Everglades, she would push him out of the plane. If the fall didn't kill him, the crocodiles would.

Actually, the dress would have been just perfect for another sort of woman — one of the young lovelies who'd appeared in *Bimbos from Satan's Spa*, for instance. The style was quite simple — a sleeveless lightweight knit with a white leather belt. The material was something else altogether. Jamie had never seen a fabric cling to every curve and hollow quite like this did.

Nothing was left to the imagination, down to and including the pitter-patter of her angry heart.

And yes, it was pink.

Staring at her reflection in the tiny mirror, she was appalled. Her small breasts seemed to take on immense proportions, straining beneath the magnetic fabric. The candy-cane shade did horrible things to her hair, turning the delicate bronze color into a brilliant strawberry-blond. The *Miami Tribune*'s Pulitzer Prize nominee looked like a . . . a bimbo. Good heavens, what would the rest of the clothes he bought her look like?

She didn't know which was worse, this dress or the dirty clothes she had just taken off. In the end, she decided to wear the dress, simply because her other clothes smelled like a smoke bomb. At least she would be a clean bimbo.

At the bottom of the shoulder bag she found white strapless sandals and a barbaric-looking silver necklace. She quite liked the jewelry actually but couldn't bring herself to wear it. She didn't need anything calling attention to her immense-looking bosom.

She outlined her eyes with soft gray kohl, then applied foundation to hide her freckles. There was no need for rouge. Her cheeks were flaming. She hoped there were millions of hungry crocodiles in the Everglades.

Chris was reading the airline's magazine and sipping a Coke when she returned to her seat. Jamie reached above his head, shoving the shoulder tote and the makeup bag into the storage compartment. A pillow tumbled out and she tossed it into the window seat, nearly knocking the Coke out of his hand.

"Excuse me," she said. "I need to get by."

Chris stood oh-so-slowly, his eyes running the length of her, the width of her, the depth and breadth of her. Moving into the aisle, his shin hit the metal edge of his seat with a thump. He didn't feel a thing.

Jamie brushed past him, dropping into her seat. Immediately she rose again, pulled the pillow from beneath her and sat back down. She fixed her eyes on the dark void beyond the window, her fingers drumming silently on the pillow in her lap. A single star flickered weakly in the night. She made a wish, a grim little smile touching her lips. *I hope his luggage is lost and he has to buy horrible flannel shirts in Clearwater. And I hope he's allergic to flannel.*

"They didn't have a size six," Chris said

huskily. "I got you a four." The busy little drink cart came rolling by again, nudging him back into his seat. He still held his Coke in one hand and the magazine in the other. He had forgotten both.

He wondered if she had any idea what she was doing to him. His pulse was frantic. His skin had grown hot, as if he had a fever. He'd known the dress would become her. It was bright and sexy and bold, which was exactly how he saw Jamie. He hadn't realized, however, what the dress would do to *him*. He wasn't prepared for the excitement, the hunger, the urgency that struck him inside like a blow.

"I'm terrified," Jamie said suddenly.

Startled, Chris tore his eyes away from her and glanced out the window. As far as he could see, the 747 still had both wings and none of the engines were on fire. His gaze returned to Jamie. She didn't look terrified. She looked beautiful, distant, and preoccupied.

Chris's instincts told him to tread lightly. In his experience, a thoughtful woman was a dangerous woman. "What do you mean, you're terrified?"

Still she stared out the window, a little muscle working in her cheek. "Sooner or later," she said slowly, "I'm going to have to look inside that big suitcase of mine. The thought absolutely terrifies me."

He tapped her gently on the shoulder. "Would you mind looking at me when you speak to me? There. That's better. Are you trying to tell me you don't like my taste in women's clothes?"

"I look sleazy."

He grinned, slowly, deliciously. "You look fantastic. That dress was made for you. Why didn't you wear the necklace with it?"

"I didn't want to call attention to my . . . never mind. Why pink? Didn't you hear me tell you I never wear pink?"

"I thought you would look nice in pink."

He seemed sincere. He certainly looked sincere, with that boyish smile lingering about his eyes and the corners of his lips. Jamie subsided into a brooding silence. Two days ago she'd had her life completely under control. She'd had a nice home, a really nice home. She'd had a closet full of simple, sporty clothes, not a one of them pink. She'd had a beautiful four-poster bed with a soft, lumpy mattress that fit her perfectly. She'd had a nifty little microwave that fit snugly beneath her kitchen cupboards. And she'd had an entire collection of Katharine Hepburn movies on videotape.

"Are you all right?" Chris said quietly.

Jamie nodded. "I'm fine."

"You're crying."

She looked at him in some perplexity, then put her hand to her cheek and touched the wetness there. Tears. How strange. She hadn't even realized . . . "I'm sorry," she said tightly. She wiped her cheeks with shaky fingers. "I suppose I'm just tired."

"Tired?" Chris experienced a wave of soft anger in his chest. This independent attitude of hers was really getting on his nerves. A woman who had just lost everything she had ever owned in the world, a woman who had been arrested and fingerprinted and thrown into jail, a woman who was the target of a notorious criminal, shouldn't feel compelled to make excuses for her low spirits. A sunny disposition was not expected under the circumstances. "Why don't you admit it?" he said. "You're under a hell of a lot of pressure. You've reached your limit."

"Actually, I feel better," Jamie replied. "I guess it helps to let off some steam."

"Steam? That was steam? Well, hey, you learn something new every day." Chris jammed his magazine into the seat pocket in front of him and passed his half-empty plastic glass to the stewardess. He didn't want it. It irritated the hell out of him when she refilled it and gave it back. "When I need to let off a little steam, I throw a small appliance through a window."

"I thought you were the man who had learned to go with the flow."

"I have. And occasionally the flow is through a window. If I'm calm, I'm a pussycat. If I'm angry, I go for the toaster. It's all the same principle. You don't fight nature."

Jamie's smile was faint and wry. Yes, she could visualize Chris Hogan winging his toaster through the window. Also a blender, coffee maker, and microwave. "I imagine that gets to be kind of expensive."

"It's better than getting an ulcer," Chris said.

"How did you know I —"

"I didn't." He smiled. "Till now."

Without another word, Jamie put on her headphones, selected a soothing soft-rock station, and positioned her pillow behind her head. She didn't want to talk to her temperamental bodyguard any longer. She wanted to sleep, so she would stop doing foolish things like crying without realizing it. Tears were a sign of foolish weakness, nothing more. She hated tears.

Johnny Mathis sang her to sleep. When she opened her eyes again, the plane's interior lighting had been dimmed and Christopher Cross was singing one of her favorite songs, "Sailing." The song cast a dreamy, romantic spell. Hazy white light drifted down from recessed globes above each seat, adding to Jamie's sleepy, sensual mood. She turned her head, blinking Chris into focus. Like her, he as wearing earphones. He was asleep, his mouth parted slightly, his hair tangled softly over the Band-Aid on his forehead. There was a warm flush staining the skin below his thick sable lashes. He seemed so very young and innocent in the unguarded dishevelment of sleep. A fleeting smile touched his lips; she wondered if his dreams were sweet.

He was a contradiction upon a contradiction, this man who claimed to achieve serenity by tossing toasters through windows. His crooked smile was disarming and boyish, a sharp contrast to the weary cynicism she had seen in his eyes. Jamie had no idea how old he might be. His smile was twenty. His shadowed eyes were forty.

"Sleep well, Marlowe," she whispered, then turned her head back into her pillow and closed her eyes.

Chris wasn't asleep. Not by a long shot. He was listening to his kind of music — oldies but goodies. The Troggs were singing

"Wild Thing." What a great song. They didn't write 'em like that anymore. Simple and to the point.

He stretched and opened his eyes, glancing at his sleepy next-door neighbor in the window seat.

Yes, she definitely looked the part in that fantastic dress he'd picked out. He loved what the color did to her hair, turning it into a bright, blazing cloud. Someday Jamie Cross would thank him for introducing her to the color pink.

She sighed in her sleep, her face turning toward him. Her soft cheeks were reddened from the starched fabric of the pillow. A scattering of freckles stood out on her small, straight nose. And her mouth — her mouth was silky as a child's, dreamy and evocative. She'd surprised him with her fierce pride and her quiet courage, but it was this undefended posture that touched him the most. At this moment, all he wanted in the world was to hold her, just hold her.

He was exhibiting symptoms of tenderness. And here he'd thought life held no more surprises.

Actually "Wild Thing" was a silly song, he decided, flicking off the music and removing the headphones. No substance. From now on it was nothing but classical music. He had it on the best authority that stylish private detectives always listened to classical music.

"I'm sorry, sir, but your luggage appears to have gone on to San Francisco."

Chris stared at the bright little pixie behind Air West's passenger information desk. "I beg your pardon?"

"When you transferred to Air West in Denver, your luggage didn't." A sympathetic smile here, complete with dimples. "You continued north to Jackson Hole, your luggage went west to San Francisco. You can't believe how often this happens. Not with Air West, of course. We carry only twenty passengers on our prop jets, which enables us to offer highly personalized service. Those larger airlines simply can't keep track of what goes where, if you now what I mean. Wait a minute, and I'll find a lost luggage form. There's one around here somewhere."

Chris filled out his form, which was three pages long. While he wrote, he was acutely conscious of Jamie Cross standing beside him in her pink dress. She said absolutely nothing, although her eyes were unusually bright as she watched him fill in the endless rows of tiny boxes. He decided she was probably dumbstruck with ecstasy. It would be just like a woman to consider this some perverted case of divine justice. *Ho, ho, he bought me a sleazy pink dress when I was destitute and helpless, and now God has sent his luggage to San Francisco.*

She coughed once. Chris stared her down. "Did you say something?" he asked.

Jamie shook her head, adjusting the belt on her very pink dress. "Nothing at all, I was just clearing my throat. You know, it's one o'clock in the morning. Do you think you could speed things up a little bit?"

"Well, why on earth would I want to do that?" Chris snapped, fatigue and frustration edging his voice. "I love filling out asinine forms. It's just like being back in the police department."

Jamie opened her green eyes very wide. "My, oh my. Where's a toaster when you need one?"

It was two A.M. before they left the airport in their rental car. They were driving a red Honda Civic not much larger than Chris's Fiat. Jamie's luggage filled the back seat to overflowing.

"It's a good thing you traveled light," she said conversationally. "We really don't have room for any of your luggage, anyway."

"That makes me feel so much better."

"I suppose you'd like me to be quiet so you can concentrate on your driving."

"You're right." Jackson Hole was a ghost town at two in the morning. The night lights of the main thoroughfare flashed rainbow colors on empty streets. "This traffic is murder."

Jamie buckled her seat belt with great care, suppressing the smile that threatened.

Chris turned the Honda into the parking lot of the first motel they came to. It wasn't much — a narrow adobe building with a string of recessed doorways — but the sign read VACANCY. Jamie looked at him in surprise. "What are we doing here?" she asked.

"We're sleeping off jet lag. When I looked at that map of yours, I figured Clearwater was at least two or three hours outside of Jackson Hole. Two in the morning is a lousy time to explore the wonders of Wyoming."

Jamie stifled a yawn. "If you're worried about me, it's not necessary. I'm really not that tired. I'm actually very —"

"Strong." Chris sighed. "I know." He opened his door and the overhead light came on, illuminating Jamie's red-rimmed eyes. He smiled and touched the tip of her nose with his finger. "Why don't you humor me and stop being strong for a little while? Macho private eyes need at least six hours of sleep a night or we turn wimpy."

"If it means that much to you." This time she didn't try to hide the yawn that turned her eyes to water. Her smile was soft and sleepy.

"It means that much to me." The silence that filled the car was pleasant and easy . . . until his gaze drifted from her shining eyes to her softly parted lips. Then he lost his smile and he couldn't find it again for the life of him. That companionable silence was suddenly so thick and heavy it was difficult to breathe. "The bodyguard is always the boss," he added, wanting to look away. So why the hell couldn't he?

Jamie had sensed a dark intensity within him, carefully glossed over with a boyish smile and a dry wit. Suddenly it seemed he wasn't bothering with the civilized veneer. She saw it in his eyes, the stark masculine need. Something very primitive in him was reaching out to her, and something deep within, Jamie stirred in response.

But only for a moment. In the space of a heartbeat, Chris was smiling again, commenting on the cool August nights in Wyoming. The overhead light went off as he shut the door, then on again as he opened hers. No, she couldn't sit all alone in a dark parking lot while he checked in. Yes, he did take his job seriously. *No,* he didn't take it too seriously.

Chris requested adjoining rooms. The sleepy night clerk, too tired to be tactful, said none of their rooms had connecting doors, but the walls were so thin it was almost the same thing. He gave Chris the key for number nine, Jamie the key for ten. Chris discovered that Jamie's room was a corner unit and immediately switched keys with her.

"You've got an extra window in ten," he said on the way back to the car. "It's better I sleep there."

Jamie rolled her eyes to the Wyoming heavens. "And you claim not to take your job too seriously."

Number nine had antiseptic white walls, a sturdy double bed, and a cold tile floor. A velvet painting of an elk hung above a wooden dresser. Jamie set her makeup case on the bedside table next to the Gideon Bible. "It's very clean," she said.

Chris followed her into the room lugging the red suitcase. Immediately his attention was caught by the velvet elk. "Something tells me I should have held out for a Holiday Inn," he murmured.

"This isn't bad," Jamie said through another yawn. "It's very clean."

He smiled, swinging the suitcase up on

the bed. "It certainly is very clean. Lie down before you fall down, Jamie. If you need me" — he tapped lightly on the wall next to the bed — "just knock. Otherwise keep the door and windows locked, just as a precaution."

"Yes, sir, Mr. Bodyguard, sir." She offered a rather sloppy salute.

His smile was dreamy. "Such a funny girl. By the way, stay off the phone. Now that we're good and lost in Wyoming, we don't want anyone tracing any long-distance calls."

"Aren't you going to tuck me into bed?" Jamie asked solemnly. "Just to make sure I get there safely?" It was a joke, only a joke. His bright blue eyes pinned her against the wall, and she added faintly, "That was just a little hiding-out humor."

"I see." Chris leaned his shoulder against the door frame, wondering if she realized he actually needed the support. Tucking Jamie Cross into bed was enormously appealing. "It's nice to see you're keeping a sense of humor about all this."

She smiled. "A sense of humor is about all I have left."

"That's not true," he said reproachfully. "What about that nice big suitcase full of pink clothes?"

Jamie stared at the mysterious luggage, half-believing him. "You didn't."

Chris's attention had wandered back to the chenille bedspread. He was still preoccupied with her hiding-out humor. "Didn't what?"

"My clothes. Tell me they aren't all pink. Even if it's a lie, tell me they aren't all pink."

Chris smiled brightly, looking totally relaxed and at ease and feeling anything but. "Time to be running along," he said. He glanced at the tacky velvet painting and sighed. "I only pray I have one of those in my room. G'night, Jamie. Lock the door after me." He left with a lazy flick of his hand, closing the door firmly behind him. Jamie waited, counting silently to ten before she heard his dulcet tones from behind the door.

"Why do you have to be difficult? *Lock it.*"

Grinning to herself, she clicked the deadbolt, then fastened the security chain. Putting her mouth close to the door, she said sweetly, "You can go to bed now, Marlowe."

The motel clerk wasn't exaggerating when he'd said the walls were paper-thin. She heard Chris unlock the room next door. She also heard him flick the light switch,

71

toss the room key on the dresser, and draw the curtains. Jamie kicked off her sandals, then on impulse crawled across the bed to their adjoining wall.

"You forgot to lock your door," she said.

There was a moment of silence. Bedsprings squeaked. "Go to sleep, brat." His voice was only slightly muffled.

"I can't. You're making *way* too much noise." She stretched out on the bed, bare toes nudging the suitcase to one side. It teetered on the edge of the mattress, then hit the tile floor with a bang.

"What the hell was that?"

"Big red suitcase went boom," Jamie said.

"Hell. You gave me a coronary. Will you please try to relax?"

"I'm relaxed." Jamie looked across the room, meeting the slightly cross-eyed gaze of her velvet elk. "Do you have one?" she asked her talking wall.

There was a short silence. "One what?"

"An elk. Do you have an elk in your room?"

"No." His sigh was clearly audible. "I have a grizzly."

She brought her body an inch or two closer to the wall. "Chris?"

"Hmmm?"

"The clothes you bought me. Are they all pink?"

"Sweet Jamie." There was a smile in his voice, and something more. "Are you always this restless when you're exhausted?"

He sounded so close, as if she could reach out and touch him. Gently she placed her hand on the wall, palm down. She wondered what he was thinking, what he was feeling. Softly she said, "No. Just . . . tonight."

"Must be something in the air." His voice was barely audible.

"Must be." She visualized him lying on his back with his hands behind his head, soft hair tangled above his blue eyes. A dreamy heat spread in her, unfamiliar and intriguing. "Sweet dreams, Marlowe."

There was a long silence; she thought he might have drifted off to sleep. Then he said huskily, "Forgive me, Murphy, for I am about to sin."

Eyes wide, she listened to his door open and close. Heart thudding, she heard him knock twice on her own door.

Her legs were uncooperative. It took an eternity to cross the space from her bed to the door. Numb fingers dealt with the safety chain and the deadbolt. She opened the door slowly, clutching the cold metal knob in a white-knuckled grip.

He stood motionless, staring at her, saying nothing. His shirt was unbuttoned, hanging outside his jeans. His cheeks were stained with a hard flush. His eyes were indigo, naked and intense. She couldn't look away from those eyes.

"This is a hell of an unprofessional thing I'm going to do," he said.

She swallowed hard. "What is?"

"This." He cupped her face in his hands, and she could feel the trembling tension in his fingers. His shadowed lashes drifted over the brilliant glitter in his eyes, like a storm cloud covering the sun. He brought his face down to hers by inches, savoring every moment, every breath, every second of exquisite anticipation. Whatever the future held, this moment would never come again. He wanted to make it last forever.

His open mouth took hers gently, so gently. His kiss was tentative at first, a heady, cautious testing. Jamie was unprepared for the tenderness of his lips, for the frantic rush of feeling deep in her body as he initiated his erotic exploration. His mouth dragged over hers, tasting, touching, drawing a soft moan her throat. She had never been kissed before, Jamie thought mindlessly. Not like this, not a kiss that could leave her shivering and bewildered.

And so hungry for more.

At last he let the kiss deepen. His fingers curved under her chin to alter the angle of her head, opening her mouth to the hard stroke of his tongue. Urgency sang through Jamie's blood. Her hands ran desperately over the corded muscles in his neck and shoulders, slipped beneath his open shirt to touch the blood-hot skin over his heart. She twisted closer, her restive senses learning the feel of him. No one had ever shattered her defenses like this, moved her like this. She was sinking fast.

She felt him pushing away from her with trembling purpose. His eyes were hazy with frustrated longing. Jamie sensed that everything within him was shivering with tension, waiting to snap out of control. She also knew he wasn't the sort of man to allow himself to lose that control.

He rested his hands on her waist and buried his head in the silky warmth of her neck. "I came back to" — he paused to take a betraying breath — "make sure you were safe."

"Am I?" Jamie asked softly. She rubbed her cheek against his hair, back and forth.

"No. Not while I'm still here." He lifted his, head, lips curling in a rueful smile. "Why do you think I told you to lock your door?"

Her eyes met his. "I'll be more careful next time."

Next time. Chris remembered the white-hot fury of the bomb that had gutted her apartment. He remembered Murphy's instructions: *Your role is short and sweet. Once she's safely in Wyoming, you have nothing to worry about. Fly back home, pick up your check, and call good old Esther to celebrate.*

Protective fear for Jamie washed like acid through his veins. It wasn't going to be enough. Delivering her safely to Clearwater would not put an end to his responsibility. Returning to Miami would not sever the ties that bound him. Despite everything he had gone through, despite the scars he carried from the past, he had somehow allowed himself to become involved. And now he would never be able to protect her enough.

How had he allowed it to happen?

"You should rest now," he said.

Jamie sensed the change in him. He was so close to her, touching her hair, her cheek. At the same time his eyes were shadowed and bleak, a world away from her. "What is it?" she whispered. "What's wrong?"

Chris shook his head. "Nothing."

"Did I say something —"

"No," He dropped a cool kiss on her brow. "Sleep well. I won't be far away."

76

Jamie watched him walk away, her hands feeling empty and useless at her sides. *But you are, Chris Hogan. You're very, very far away.*

CHAPTER

Four

Jamie put it off as long as she could.

Already she'd showered, brushed her teeth, and put on a bit of makeup. She looked at the faint circles under her eyes and put on a bit more. She even made the bed where she'd tossed and turned most of the night. She never did get used to the idea of Chris Hogan sleeping inches away.

She was standing in her bra and panties staring at the red suitcase when Chris rapped on the wall. "Are you ready in there? I'd like to get going before noon."

"I'm ready," Jamie said, lifting the suitcase onto the bed. "Almost. Give me a minute."

"Sixty seconds and counting."

Jamie made a face at him through the wall. Then, with great trepidation, she opened the suitcase.

At first glance it wasn't as bad as she had feared. The clothes weren't all pink. A great many of them were, but not all. Jamie pulled out a brightly printed sundress, feeling hopeful. No. The thing was strapless, cut down to her waist in the back. She found a pair of yellow shorts that looked decent; unfortunately, the yellow knit halter top designed to go with them had *very* little to recommend it. There was a semitransparent lace and cotton minidress. There was a flowered skirt slit up to her thigh. There was an assortment of itsy-bitsy tank tops and short shorts and ruffled miniskirts.

She let out a shocking string of swear words and pounded on the wall. "Where did you *buy* these clothes, Marlowe? Frederick's of Hollywood?"

"What do you expect in eighteen minutes?"

"Where're the jeans?"

"I told you, I bought jeans. They're in there, just look. And there are some tank tops that would look absolutely —"

"I saw the tank tops!" she yelled.

"My, my. Do you always wake up this grumpy?"

Jamie dug deeper in the suitcase. She came up with two pairs of extremely heavy, extremely stiff jeans. Shrink-to-fit, naturally. She might be able to wear them after three or four washings.

"Find the jeans?" he called out.

"I'll get you for this, Chris Hogan," she muttered. "With this elk as my witness, I swear I'll get you for this."

Eventually she found a black scoop-neck

T-shirt that was only slightly revealing and a pair of khaki slacks that actually fit. Everything else went back in the suitcase in a colorful heap. She had to concentrate on unclenching her teeth. No ruffles, she'd told him. Nothing pink. Just simple, sporty clothes. And what did she get? Mata Hari's Lazy Days of Summer Collection.

She opened her motel room door just as Chris raised his hand to knock.

"You look very nice," he said, sounding a bit disappointed. His yellow shirt was somewhat the worse for two day's wear, and a dark beard shadowed the square line of his jaw. "Did you see the flowered sundress?"

"I saw it," Jamie said shortly.

"What about the pink miniskirt —"

"I saw it, too. I saw *everything*." She shoved the suitcase over the threshold. "I haven't decided if you're a sadist, a lecher, or a simple-minded man with execrable taste in women's clothes."

"Maybe you didn't see the yellow shorts set." He saw the answer in her eyes and grimaced. "Didn't like that either, huh? Oh, well. There's no accounting for taste."

"Exactly what I've been thinking," Jamie muttered, glaring at him. His boyish expression said plaintively, *It isn't my fault. What does an ex-cop know about women's fashions?*

She wasn't fooled for a minute.

They drove three blocks to Ruth & Nick's Diner. Chris ordered bacon and eggs, hash brown potatoes, whole wheat toast, and coffee. Jamie ordered Cream of Wheat.

"If you'd throw a few toasters around," Chris said helpfully, "you wouldn't have to baby that ulcer. You need to learn to release your hostilities."

Jamie regarded him thoughtfully. "Since I'm feeling a little . . . *hostile* at the moment, what would you have me do?"

Blue eyes gleamed beneath heavy lids. "That kind of depends on whom your hostility is directed toward."

"For the sake of conversation, let's say . . . you."

His wide mouth tilted at the corners with a smile. "Oh. Well, if you follow the example of the rest of your sex when they get a little hostile, you'd probably haul off and slap me."

"Would I?" Keeping her eyes locked on his, she raised her hand slowly in the air. "Are you sure this is going to make me feel better?" she asked innocently.

"Abusing men has always made women feel better."

"Right here in public?"

"It's only truly effective in public."

Jamie looked at him with her huge green eyes. "So tempting," she said, wriggling her upraised fingers. "Heaven knows you deserve it. Fortunately I'm a forgiving person." But when she would have dropped her hand, his fingers curved around her wrist, holding it there.

"That's what causes ulcers," he said with the air of someone imparting a great bit of wisdom. "I can see you need a little help releasing your pent-up frustrations. First, bear in mind that a hostile woman seldom hits the thing she aims for. I would suggest you aim for my jaw." He drew her hand toward him, placing her palm on the curve of his cheek. "That way you'll probably whack me in the eye. There's nothing more satisfying for a woman than giving a man a black eye." He thought that over and frowned. "Nothing you can do in public, anyway."

Jamie's palm tingled. She could feel the velvet-rough stubble along his jaw, the hard plane of his cheekbone, the warmth of his skin. She met his sparkling gaze with difficulty. This couldn't be good for her ulcer.

"I need my hand back," she said huskily. "My Cream of Wheat is getting cold."

"I wouldn't want that to happen," he

said. Still holding her wrist, he turned his head fractionally, touching the center of her palm with his tongue. Before Jamie could find her breath, his lips replaced his tongue, closing over the ultra-sensitive skin in a gentle, warm sucking motion.

Jamie closed her eyes briefly, catching her lower lip between her teeth. "Let go," she whispered, knowing full well she could free herself any time she chose. "This is embarrassing."

"This is therapeutic." His breath tickled over her damp skin. He grinned, twin fires burning in his hooded eyes. "I'm teaching you to relax, to give that clever little mind of yours a rest now and again. Go with the flow, Jamie — remember?"

At the moment, the flow was prickling and sparking up and down her body. In the tips of her fingers. In the pulse at her temples. And deep within the core of her abdomen . . .

"I think it's safer to be neurotic," she said huskily, pulling her hand away. "And I want my cereal." And how appetizing it looked, clotted and rubbery in a bath of lukewarm milk. She forced herself to take a spoonful, swallowing the puttylike lumps with visible effort. "Just what my ulcer ordered."

Chris bit into a piece of crisp bacon,

eyeing her thoughtfully. "You're a difficult woman to relax."

Jamie had to smile, thinking of his methods. "I'm a lost cause, Marlowe. I never really learned how to relax. Now and then I fall into unconsciousness when I've been working on a column for three days straight. That's about as close as I ever get to total relaxation."

"Fortunately, you now have a professional to guide you," he replied. His smile was as pure as the driven snow.

She matched him smile for smile. "I guess I'll just have to survive without your expertise. In a few hours you'll be winging your way back to Miami, remember? Think of me in the days to come when you're doing all the fun things private eyes do. I'll probably be sitting on the front porch of some rustic hideaway, whittling. That should be relaxing."

This irritated him. With apparent indifference, she had reminded him that their time was running out. He was painfully aware of his own resistance to the idea. "I doubt you know any more about whittling than you know about private investigators."

She shrugged. "So tell me. Just how does a private eye — excuse me, investigator — spend his days?"

"Oh, it's fascinating stuff," Chris said. "I stake out the sleazy motels in town, taking pictures of naughty businessmen. I've gotten to be quite handy with the old camera. Let's see, what else? I deliver summonses. I've done some work for insurance companies, investigating bogus whiplash claims and back injuries. Now and then I do a little muckraking for a couple of divorce attorneys I know. There's never a dull moment in the private eye business." Suddenly he became aware of the acute perception in her eyes, and his lips tightened. He hadn't meant to reveal quite so much of himself.

"Did you enjoy police work?" Jamie asked curiously.

"It had its moments."

"But you resigned?"

"Yes."

"After eleven years?"

"Yes. Would you like some coffee?"

"Why did you resign?"

"You know, for a minute there, I forgot you were a reporter." He threw her an exasperated look. "Why don't you finish your Cream of Wheat, Ace? We've got a long drive ahead of us."

The planet Wyoming took Jamie by surprise. This wide-open country was unlike anything she had ever seen. There were terrifying mountains, rumpled green hills, shaggy forests, and noisy waterfalls spilling over jagged white rocks. The roads were narrow and inconsistent. They never followed a straight line — they snaked around in circles and dips and switchbacks that accommodated the unaccommodating terrain. In Miami, after spending an hour on the highways, you *arrived* somewhere. In Wyoming, it seemed that there was always another bubbling river to cross, another lake to circle, another furry green meadow waiting to swallow the little Honda. And there wasn't a single taxi in sight.

"I'm beginning to understand how Dorothy must have felt," Jamie remarked. They had stopped to allow an enormous milk cow the right of way as it crossed the road. Jamie thought it extremely odd that milk cows were allowed to run wild here. In Miami, a milk cow strolling across the interstate would be a media event.

"Dorothy who?" Chris asked absently. He was imagining the damage an animal of that size could inflict on a little Honda.

"Dorothy . . ." She paused, wrinkling her nose. "I don't know her last name. Dorothy in *The Wizard of Oz*. She knew if she followed the yellow brick road long enough, eventually she would get to Oz. But she had no idea how long it would take or what strange things waited for her around the bend."

Chris stared at the cow's swollen udders. "I know what you mean."

Faintly Jamie said, "Some people would probably enjoy this rugged atmosphere. Shaggy beasts and whatnot. Raging rivers lapping at the road. Air that smells like car freshener."

A suppressed smile flirted at the edges of his lips. "If I didn't know better, I'd think you weren't looking forward to your little vacation."

"I'll tell you a secret." Jamie tipped her head back on the seat, glancing at him through shaded lashes. "I give myself six, maybe seven days at the most in this unspoiled paradise before I go through concrete withdrawal. Then it's back to Miami. I wasn't cut out to be a fugitive. I need people to argue with, red lights to run, traffic jams to swelter in."

"Bombs to dodge?" Chris said tonelessly.

"At least life won't be boring."

"True. On the other hand, it may not be long, either." The cow finally plodded off into a green pasture. Chris jammed the car into gear, the tires spitting gravel behind them. He told himself this was how private detectives suffered nervous breakdowns. They became personally involved with beautiful clients who preferred TNT to TLC.

Jamie glanced sideways at his icy expression. Shadowed eyes, skin drawn tight over his cheekbones. She'd upset him again. Probably it would have been wise to keep her fugitive phobia to herself. She turned to the window, pretending great interest in the green blur beyond. "You're zipping right along on these twists and turns, aren't you? It's amazing how close you can come to the edge of the road without actually going off."

He jerked the wheel to avoid a flat, furry something in the road. "All those car chases from my cops and robber days must have paid off."

Jamie twisted in her seat, trying to identify the lifeless mass disappearing behind them. "What was that?"

"Road pancake."

Her startled gaze swung quickly back to him. "Thank you. I suppose you couldn't think of a less repulsive way to phrase that?"

"Squashed porcupine," he snapped.

Obviously the flow was a little temperamental today. Jamie took a deep breath and tried again. "So how long do you think it will take us to reach Clearwater?"

Chris concentrated on relaxing the corded muscles in his neck and back. He was overreacting. The truth of the matter was, his job was nearly over. After today, Jamie was on her own. She could choose to take up whittling, decide to climb the Grand Tetons in high heels, or return to Miami. He would hardly be able to influence her — or protect her — from three thousand miles away. She was an adult and capable of accepting the consequences of her own actions. It was time he accepted the fact.

"We shouldn't be too long now." He loosened his grip on the steering wheel, finger by finger. He even managed a stiff little smile. "Anxious to be rid of me, are you?"

"Actually" — Jamie closed her eyes as they swooped into another tree-shaded hollow — "I'm anxious to get out of this car — I feel like I've been on a two-hour rollercoaster ride. I've never been real good on roller coasters."

"Ask and you shall receive." Chris nodded his head, indicating the green valley that had suddenly opened up before them. It looked like a patchwork quilt, with meadows and pastures and fields of various textures and colors. A white church steeple was visible above a rolling stand of pines. "Unless I've read Murphy's map wrong — which is highly unlikely, ex-bloodhound that I am — that picturesque community is Clearwater, Wyoming, home to fugitive journalists."

Jamie swallowed hard on nothing. Clearwater might have been a reincarnation of Walton's Mountain. She could picture an exuberant John Boy riding a mule across the emerald green fields, his little straw hat blowing off behind him. This was an unspoiled paradise of peace, serenity, and well-being. As a fugitive journalist, she found it unnerving to be suddenly in an oasis of calm. A restless soul such as her own did not take well to utter tranquility.

Somewhat forlornly she said, "It's very pretty."

Reading her mind, Chris patted her sympathetically on the shoulder. "Cheer up, Ace. With you around, Clearwater couldn't possibly be dull. Maybe there'll be a forest fire or something. Hope on, hope ever. Now keep your eyes open for a gravel lane with a wooden gate. Murphy said the house was set back a couple of hundred feet from the road."

Faintly, "It's not actually in the town, then?"

"Just outside."

90

Wonderful. Isolation *and* tranquility. Jamie found some aspirin in her purse and swallowed them dry.

Bloodhound that he was, Chris drove straight to the house as if he'd lived there all his life. Tangled knee-high lengths of grass surrounded the A-frame log structure. A covered porch ran the length of the house, shading a faded canvas swing and several plastic lawn chairs. A hand-painted sign above the front door proclaimed this CAPWELL'S HOMESTEAD.

"Capwell's," Chris said with no little satisfaction. "Just like the map says. I amaze myself sometimes, I really do. After you, madam. Your rustic mountain hideaway awaits."

Jamie plastered a smile on her face and threw open the car door. The air was filled with hot sunlight and the electric hum of insects. Water splashed and gurgled somewhere in the shadow of the pine trees. A red-eyed rabbit stared at her from beneath the front porch.

She ascended the steps slowly, Chris following behind. Despite the weatherbeaten look of the wood, everything seemed in good repair. The stairs were sturdy. The diamond-paned windows on either side of the front door were sparkling clean.

"The Bates Motel probably had clean windows, too," Jamie muttered.

"What's that?"

"Did you ever see *Psycho*?"

Chris gave her a lopsided grin. "Poor baby. It must be exhausting, having the imagination of a writer. The key's supposed to be in the window box on the left."

Jamie found the key and jammed it into the lock. "It doesn't work."

"You've got it upside down."

"I knew that."

A short tour of the cottage laid Anthony Perkins's ghost to rest. The rooms were small but cozily furnished in a casual, haphazard style. A huge stone fireplace added atmosphere to the living area, which was divided from the bright little kitchen by a handmade bar of polished teak. Jamie was not entirely familiar with the appliances in the kitchen. A minuscule icebox beneath the hardwood counter apparently substituted for a side-by-side refrigerator-freezer. An enormous black iron stove squatted in the corner, mysterious and forbidding. No toaster. No blender. No electric can opener. Jamie began to chew her nails.

"I put your luggage in the bedroom," Chris said behind her.

Jamie jumped. "Don't sneak up on me

like that. I'm adjusting."

He smiled. "To what?"

"The quiet life." She couldn't help noticing that Chris seemed restless. Thumbs hooked in his pockets, he shifted his weight from one foot to the other, his gaze skipping from window to window in the living room. "I suppose you're anxious to leave," she said, feeling an odd little pang somewhere in the region of her heart. She tried not to stare at him too overtly. Contrasted with the beard shadow on his jaw, his eyes were diamond-bright, softened with a sunburst of tiny lines at each corner. Lost in those eyes, Jamie experienced a bittersweet blend of yearning and remembered passion.

She missed him already.

"There doesn't seem to be anything else for me to do here," he said brusquely. Heaven knew he'd searched for an excuse to stay with her another hour, another day. He'd double-checked the locks on the doors and windows, hoping for a broken latch that would require his attention. He'd even inspected the plumbing in the bathroom. With his plumbing experience — or lack of it — a simple leaky faucet could take a full week to repair. Unfortunately, everything appeared to be in tip-top shape. Damn it all.

"There's no telephone," he said. "I'd feel

better if you had a telephone."

Jamie shrugged. "Don't worry about it."

"I'm not worried. I'd just feel better if I could check on you, that's all."

"I'll be fine."

"Fine." He raked a hand through his tumbled hair. "There seems to be nothing more for me to do, then."

"So" — Jamie's voice was oddly husky — "where do we go from here?"

He met her eyes. Silence whispered around then, "I suppose we drive to Clearwater," he said finally. "I'm leaving the Honda with you, so I need to rent another car. Besides, you need to pick up some food and supplies."

"Clearwater's a fairly small town. What if there isn't any place to rent a —"

"There is," Chris said flatly. "Murphy already arranged it. He didn't want to pay me overtime while I thumbed a ride back to Jackson Hole."

"Oh." Still locked in his gaze, Jamie felt her heart slipping into her throat. He looked at her for what seemed to be an eternity, quietly and patiently, though not without a trace of urgency. Gradually a shadow of what might have been anger clouded his eyes.

"It's time to go," he said. He pulled the

car keys from his pocket and tossed them to her. "You may as well drive. You do understand the mysterious workings of a clutch and gearshift?"

"I think I can manage."

"Fine."

"Fine."

It may have been the sun that blinded her when she marched outside. It may have been her preoccupation with the frustration and confusion that threatened her dry eyes and plastic smile. Whatever the reason, Jamie took two steps in the long grass and suddenly lost her balance. She plunged headfirst in the waxy spears of grass, both hands automatically reaching to break her fall. She came down hard, her nose in a rabbit hole and one wrist bent backward beneath her chest.

Chris was beside her in an instant, touching her shoulders, her back. "Jamie? Are you all right? Talk to me, Jamie!"

He was probing in all the wrong places. Jamie rolled over onto her back, gasping at the white-hot pain stabbing through her wrist. "I don't . . . feel . . . like talking."

"Where are you hurt?"

"You mean besides my pride?" The grass was unbelievably stiff, scratching her arms and neck. She managed to sit up, cradling her wrist in her good arm. "I think I broke my wrist." It was already swelling, a red-hot flush building beneath the skin. "*Damn.* I need this like I need milk cows and fresh air."

"Let me look." He pushed gently at the angry swelling, and she caught her lip between her teeth. "I think it's broken," he said.

Jamie fought the tears that burned her eyes. "Thank you. I needed a second opinion."

"Well, you're going to get a third opinion." Effortlessly he scooped her up in his arms, being careful not to jar her wrist. She seemed to weigh absolutely nothing. "There's got to be a doctor in Clearwater. That wrist needs to be X-rayed."

Jamie sniffed. "Maybe we can find a veterinarian. Maybe he'll shoot me and put me out of my misery."

Chris brushed a gentle kiss on her forehead with all the new tenderness in his soul. "And here you thought Clearwater was going to be dull."

There was indeed a doctor in Clearwater. The attendant at the local gas station directed them to a white clapboard house on First Street, located across the street from the post office and next door to the Dairy Queen. A metal sign swung from a wrought-iron post in the overgrown front yard.

"Casey Fletcher, M.D.," Jamie muttered, reading the faded black lettering. She glanced at the mud-splattered Jeep Renegade in the driveway. "I've never known a doctor named Casey. This should be interesting."

The front office was rather tame. A middle-aged woman with pale blue hair sat behind the desk, knitting needles clicking away. She fussed sympathetically over Jamie's poor wrist, gave Chris a metal clipboard with several forms to fill out, and whisked the new patient into an examining room.

"Casey will be with you in a moment," she said cheerfully. "If you'll just sit up here on the examining table — that's right. You're lucky he's in. He just got back from the hospital in Pinedale." She paused for air, studying Jamie with unabashed curiosity. "Are you married, dear?"

"No." Jamie wondered what sort of nurse called a doctor by his first name.

"How interesting." She gave Jamie a pillow to elevate her wrist. "I'll tell Casey you're here."

There was a Norman Rockwell print

hanging on the wall. Staring at it, trying to take her mind off her throbbing wrist, Jamie had to smile. A curly-haired farm boy in jeans and a straw hat was carefully measuring cough medicine for his sick puppy. The sleepy-eyed dog was tucked snugly into a cardboard box and covered with a red baby blanket.

Suddenly the door swung open and a tall, dark-haired man strode in. "You're smiling," he announced. "You can't be too sick if you're smiling. I'm Casey Fletcher."

Now Jamie had something else to take her mind off her wrist. Dr. Casey Fletcher. He wore cowboy boots, faded blue jeans, and a blue chambray shirt. His glossy, dark brown hair was swept back from his face, hanging nearly to his shoulders. His eyes were the color of strong coffee, twinkling in his sun-bronzed face. He couldn't have been more than thirty-two or thirty-three years old.

"You're my doctor," Jamie said, the statement coming out more as a question.

"Yeah." He grinned, showing off matching dimples. "This is a real treat for me. Usually I work on horses."

Twenty minutes later, Chris tossed a stack of forms on the front desk. "I'm finished," he said grimly. "Now, unless you'd like me to write an essay on what I did during my summer vacation, I'd really like to see Jamie."

The knitting needles paused in midair. "I'm sorry, she's still with the doctor. Why don't you read a magazine while you wait?"

"Because I have eyestrain from filling out twelve dozen forms. Which room?"

"Look here, you've made me drop a stitch." She sighed, looking at Chris over the rim of her glasses. "Room three, down the hall and to the right."

Chris wasn't quite sure what he expected. Perhaps a white-haired old gentleman with apple-red cheeks and a stethoscope necklace. The smell of antiseptic. Norman Rockwell prints hanging on the wall.

Walking into the examining room, he saw he had two out of three right. The room did smell faintly of antiseptic. There were Norman Rockwell prints on the wall. But the long-haired cowboy rolling an Ace bandage around Jamie's wrist bore more resemblance to Jesse James than Marcus Welby.

"Chris!" Jamie smiled at him, the pupils of her eyes so dilated they all but eclipsed the irises. "I thought I'd lost you. This is my doctor, Casey Fletcher. He says I'm not broken, just sprained." She watched while Chris and Casey shook hands. "The nurse just calls him Casey 'cause she used to know him when he was two feet tall."

Chris noticed the good doctor was wearing a silver belt buckle that proclaimed him Wyoming's All-Around Cowboy of 1986. "You grew up around here?" he said slowly.

"Born and raised," Casey said. He noticed Chris staring at his belt buckle and grinned. "Don't worry. I rode the rodeo circuit for a few years, but I also managed to fit in medical school."

"He's a good doctor," Jamie testified. "He won't let me call him Dr. Fletcher, though. He says he gets a new gray hair every time a pretty woman calls him Dr. Fletcher. He gave me a shot. My wrist is fine." As a matter of fact, she felt fine all over. She smiled at Chris, feeling perfectly in control of the situation. "Everything is just fine. You can go back to Miami just like you planned."

Casey looked pointedly at Chris. "Jamie tells me she's vacationing at the Capwell place."

Chris nodded. "We are. I mean, she is."

"Her wrist is badly sprained. I gave her something for the pain — witness those glassy green eyes — but she shouldn't be left alone."

"I'm perfectly fine," Jamie said. "There's

no need for him to stay with me. He wants to get back to Miami and his camera."

"I'm going to give her a prescription for pain pills," Casey went on. "Believe me, she'll need them for a couple of days. And for the next twenty-four hours the hand should be kept elevated with an ice pack on it."

Jamie frowned. "Why are you telling *him?* He won't be here."

"Something tells me he will," Casey replied.

Chris looked at Jamie, then back to Casey. Ever so slowly his blue eyes tucked at the corners with a smile. "Something tells me you're right."

Five

DIARY OF A FUGITIVE
Day One

Technically speaking, I suppose this is Day Two. I don't remember much of yesterday. I had the misfortune of tripping over — or into — a rabbit hole. I sprained my wrist, or so said Clearwater's cheerful country doctor with the shoulder-length hair and dazzling dimples. He took away my pain with a shot of Demerol — also my memory. I snoozed in the car while Chris ran in to the drugstore for my prescription. Came to briefly when he carried me into the cabin. Nothing more.

I woke up this morning wearing my underwear and an Ace bandage. I will assume I undressed myself in my sleep. My head aches. My wrist is throbbing. My ulcer is crying. I don't know where Chris is. The Honda and the private eye are missing.

I hate rabbits and I hate being a fugitive.

Jamie put down her pen, staring at the spidery scrawl on the yellow legal tablet. It might have been Arabic or Chinese, but it certainly didn't look like English. Her left hand had no idea how to hold a pen, let alone write. Neither did her left hand know how to brush her hair, apply makeup, or fasten buttons. Jamie was forecasting several days of inadequate personal grooming.

Since waking to the obscenely bright morning, Janie's activities had been extremely limited. She had walked to the bedroom window and discovered that the car was missing, and she had visited the bathroom. Then it was back to bed, where she battled with pen and paper and her uncoordinated left hand. A full hour of concentrated effort resulted in a single page of illegible writing.

Jamie was discouraged and hungry and irritable. After sitting cross-legged on her bed for so long, she was also bloodless from the waist down. She tiptoed across the room to the window, wincing and gasping as the pins and needles shivered over her legs. Still no Honda. Obviously no Chris. He had probably driven back into Clearwater for the supplies they had never picked up yesterday. She could sit in her underwear the rest of the day feeling sorry for herself, or she could shower and dress and try to find something to eat.

Feeling as rotten as she did, it wasn't an easy decision. She forced herself to shower in ice-cold water, holding her injured hand up and out of the spray. Wrapped in a towel and goosebumps, she struggled with the lock on the red suitcase for ten minutes before managing to open it. Modesty had no bearing on her choice of clothing. She dressed in a pair of yellow shorts with an elasticized waistband and a tank top that slipped easily over her head. Once she had pulled a comb through her wet hair, she felt extremely accomplished. Not bad for a left-handed fugitive with a Demerol hangover.

The living room was full of dusty sunlight and echoing silence. A pillow on the sofa still bore the imprint of Chris's head. A tangled knot of sheets and blankets had been spread halfway across the room. Apparently the private eye had spent a less than restful night.

Jamie found several cans of pork and beans in the cupboard, along with a half-empty box of crackers. The icebox was empty. She nibbled on crackers and water, trying not to think about the scorpion pain in her wrist. She had taken her last aspirin yesterday. If only she knew where Chris had put her . . .

Prescription. Her eyes fell on the small

plastic container on the windowsill above the sink. The directions said to take two tablets with meals. Jamie knew three crackers and a glass of water hardly constituted a meal. Sensible fugitive that she was, she took only one tablet.

Jamie was sitting on the front steps of the cabin when Chris returned. He was amazed at how well she looked. Her eyes were brilliant, her color was high, her expression placid and serene. She was wearing a pair of yellow shorts that exposed a tantalizing length of beautifully tanned flesh. And the tank top — the tank top fit just as Chris had imagined . . . like yellow Saran Wrap.

What excellent taste he had.

He left the groceries in the car and joined her on the steps. "Good morning, bright eyes. You look like sunshine today."

"That's a very nice thing to say." She smiled at him, twisting a damp strand of hair around her finger. There was something different about him this morning. It took her a full minute to realize he was wearing a new shirt. And new jeans. "You're clean," she said. "Nice shirt."

Chris glanced down at his all-purpose solid blue T-shirt. "It was either this or a flannel cowboy shirt. I bought three — red, white, and blue."

His jeans were stone washed and fit him like a soft denim glove. Jamie had never, *ever* seen a pair of jeans that fit quite so well. She sighed deeply. "Nice pants, Marlowe."

He gave her a peculiar look. Something was wrong here. Cautiously he asked, "How's your wrist feeling?"

"Splendid." She patted the Ace bandage, feeling no pain. "I had a little breakfast and took a little pill."

Slowly the troubled frown between his brows smoothed out. Of course. Dr. Casey's happy pills. "What exactly did you have for your little breakfast?"

"This and that," Jamie replied airily. "Crackers. Water. You can't imagine how relieved I was to find that prescription. My wrist hurt like bloody hell this morning." She clapped her left hand over her mouth too late to stifle a giggle. " 'Scuse me. I don't usually swear."

Happy pills on an empty stomach. He should have guessed. He lifted her chin with his hand, his thumb stroking the sun-warmed skin beneath her cheekbone. "Are you having a nice trip?" Chris asked gently.

Jamie stared at him for a moment, looking up into his face with a perplexed frown. Then she gave him a sweetly lopsided smile.

"Oh, yes. I suppose I am. Do you know what I've been doing this morning?"

"Tell me," he said, touching the damp silk of her hair. He couldn't seem to stop touching her. Light and heat poured from the steel-blue sky, brushing over the dusty-gold tips of her lashes, the delicate arch of her cheekbones, the sun-flushed skin of her shoulders. In a low tone that had a slightly breathless quality to it, he repeated, "Tell me what you've been doing."

Her eyes sparkled with diamonds and sunlight. "I've been observing the wildlife. Look there." She pointed to the long grass near a shadowy cluster of pines. "See the yellow flowers near the tree stump? Look just left of there."

He looked. He saw two pink eyes, a twitching nose, and floppy ears. "It's a rabbit. You've been bunny-watching?"

"Uh-huh."

He smiled. "You like soft cuddly things?"

"Not exactly." She pulled a strand of grass from between the steps and nibbled on it. "I haven't eaten a good meal since . . . oh, I suppose since breakfast yesterday. I tasted rabbit once at a gourmet restaurant. It was wonderful, sort of like chicken. It would probably be really good fried, too." She sighed, her expression dreamy. "I've been watching that bunny and thinking about all the ways I could cook him. Stewed, baked, fricasseed . . ."

He helped her to her feet and led her gently into the cabin. Obviously she needed tender loving care. Under ordinary circumstances he was quite sure she would never consider fricasseeing Thumper. He gave her a cracker and told her to sit on the couch until he had the groceries unloaded. And then, because she was completely irresistible in her overmedicated condition, he leaned down and kissed her. Just once . . . yet he forgot how to breathe in the stress of feeling her lips opening beneath his. He pulled away before she could guess how close he was to the borderline. He had absolutely no idea how long he could subdue his need for her. Self-control was suddenly becoming a guessing game.

He intended to cook a couple of steaks for lunch, but the damn stove wouldn't cooperate. It didn't take a genius to figure out that the cast-iron monster demanded wood for its great black belly. Chris gathered up the last of the firewood from the back porch and tossed it in the stove, along with match after match after match. Every time, the same thing would happen. The matches would burn beautifully. The wood remained cold.

"I'm starving," Jamie said from her assigned position on the sofa. "Couldn't we eat something that doesn't need to be cooked?"

"I never give up," Chris muttered. He began shredding paper towels and throwing them on top of the wood.

"Couldn't you give up this once?" Jamie pleaded, "I won't think less of you, I promise. How about a bologna sandwich?"

Even with the aid of a dozen paper towels, the wood refused to burn. Chris finally fixed peanut butter and jam sandwiches, promising steaks for supper. Jamie spared a not-so-hopeful glance at the cold iron stove and murmured a noncommittal, "We'll see." She didn't really care one way or another. She was still feeling extraordinarily warm and safe and happy.

Chris was feeling extraordinarily frustrated. The cabin seemed to be closing in around them, growing smaller and more intimate with every smile Jamie threw his way. He was well aware she was floating on cloud nine, but it didn't make it any easier to moderate his immediate desire. He was dazzled by the luxurious fall of her hair as it shimmered over her bare shoulders. She laughed, and his mouth went dry. She touched his hand and his skin burned.

What would the pioneers have done? he wondered desperately. What sort of distractions could be found in this quiet wilderness?

He remembered the ax on the back porch. Of course. The universal antidote to sexual frustration. Sweat. He pushed his chair back from the table. "I'm going to chop some firewood."

Jamie's eyes opened wide. "You're what?"

"Firewood. It got a little chilly in here last night. It would be nice to have some firewood."

Jamie frowned, licking the peanut butter from her fingers. "I don't know why you want to chop more wood," she said philosophically. "You can't burn the stuff you've got."

He slammed the screen door when he left.

Shrugging, Jamie occupied herself with a little left-handed puttering in the kitchen. "Putter, putter," she said, taking the dirty dishes to the sink. "Peanut butter putter." She giggled, trying to screw the lid on the peanut butter jar with one hand. It was impossible, and quite amusing.

But one couldn't be amused by a peanut butter jar forever. Eventually the sound of steel sinking into wood drew her to the front porch. Jamie stood motionless in the cool shadows, absorbing the full impact of Chris Hogan chopping wood. His navy blue T-shirt dangled from the overhanging branch of an aspen tree. He was standing over a ragged tree stump, wielding the heavy ax as if he had been chopping wood every day of his life. With every stroke, sunlight and sweat glittered over the naked flesh of his back and chest. His powerful arm muscles bulged, the ax swung down with a metallic glint, and slivers of wood danced in the air. His hair, darkened with perspiration, was tangled in straight lengths over his forehead and ears. He shook it back from his face, wiping the sweat from his brow.

Feeling curiously light-headed, Jamie watched Chris split the logs one after another. The powerful rhythm fascinated her. The man with the cloudy blue eyes and sleek brown skin overwhelmed her. Her smile tightened and her breath came in hard little catches. She was trembling.

Chris finally buried the ax in the tree stump, then turned his head and met her gaze. His eyes narrowed against the harsh white light. Slowly he wiped his palms on the soft denim that molded his thighs. Then he turned and walked to the rusty iron pump at the side of the porch. He worked the handle several times, ducking his head and shoulders under the cold stream of water. He shook out his hair, spraying Jamie with sparkling droplets.

"Sorry," he said, watching her lick the moisture from her lips.

"Tastes good," Jamie whispered. "I'm . . . hot."

Chris closed his eyes briefly. "Oh, Jamie . . . you are so damned . . . look, I think I'll go for a walk. Why don't you go inside and sleep off that pain pill?"

Huskily, Jamie asked, "So damned what?"

His smile came slowly and didn't quite reach his eyes. "Sweet," he said softly. "So damned sweet."

"You know the nice thing about pain pills?" She leaned over the porch rail, propping her chin in her left hand. Her hair swung from the shadows into the sun, glittering with fire and life. "They give you an excuse to say anything that comes into your head."

Chris stared at the young face above him with quiet intensity. "I thought you did that anyway."

"Possibly," she conceded. "But today I don't need to feel guilty about it. Today it's perfectly natural."

His throat constricted. "What is?"

"The way I feel," she said softly. She couldn't take her eyes off the triangle of hair on his chest that glittered with water diamonds. The lean, muscular expanse of naked flesh looked so beautiful to her. "The way you make me feel. Wild and dreamy and warm." And then she smiled. "And sweet. Like a peach in the hot sun."

Chris's chest lifted with a hard, concussive breath. "Oh, hell."

"Why are you way down there?" she whispered.

"Because I'm scared to come up there."

"Don't be scared of me. I'm harmless."

"I'm not," Chris said hoarsely. In the space between his last heartbeat and his next, there was a decision to be made. And it was harder than he'd ever imagined. "Go inside, Jamie."

She shook her head. "It's lonely in there."

So she was going to be difficult. Well, what else had he expected? Even when she was clear-headed, Jamie enjoyed turmoil and upheaval. Laced with painkillers, she was terrifying.

He took the porch steps two at a time, grabbed her good hand, and pulled her into the house. "You're going to have a nap, sweetheart."

"I never have naps," Jamie protested.

"And I'm never noble and self-sacrificing." He walked into the bedroom, tugging her behind him. "There's a first time for everything."

"You're ruining my mood."

"Well, thank the Lord for small favors." Both hands on her shoulders, he pushed her gently down on the bed. "Sleep. When you wake up, the pill will have worn off and you won't feel like a peach anymore. I guarantee it."

"Can you guarantee I'll sleep?" Jamie asked. She stood up again, slipping her arms around his shoulders. Beneath her fingers, she felt his muscles jerk and tense. "You need to learn to relax, Marlowe."

His hands were on her waist, then moving in hungry patterns up and down her back. He couldn't help it, they had a mind of their own. "You're not helping me any, angel."

"Oh, I'll help you," she whispered. She was caught up in the colors of his eyes, in the starburst of gray and black that edged his pupils. "I'll help you *so* good . . ."

He felt her lashes touch his skin, her mouth whisper an endearment over his lips. Then he was kissing her with a fierce need that obliterated reason. All the tension and strain and introspection of the past few days suddenly evolved into a frenzy of desire. He wanted her, he wanted to hold her so close and so tightly he would never have to let her go. He'd been missing her all his life. No matter how close he pulled her, he couldn't ease the painful yearning in his muscles.

His spread fingers supported her back, lowering her to the bed. He came down to her with urgent heat, saying her name in a ragged whisper. She moved her hips helplessly beneath him, showering his face and hair and chest with hungry kisses.

He broke from her briefly, his skin flushed and tight over his cheekbones, his eyes hypnotically brilliant. "Your wrist . . ."

"My wrist is fine." She tangled her fingers in his hair, pulling him back to her. "I don't even feel my wrist."

It began then, even as he moved his hand beneath the soft fabric of her shirt. The cold whisper of conscience. His searching fingers discovered the aching weight of her breasts, felt the wild throbbing of her heart. So hot, she felt so hot . . .

I feel wild and dreamy and warm . . .

"I can't hurt you, Jamie." His hands cradled her head, soothing her restless movements. He gazed at the reckless stain on her cheeks, the eyes that were drenched with fever-bright color. "I can't hurt you. I can't take the chance. If you had regrets, if you had guilt, it would destroy me."

She touched his lips with trembling fingers. "Don't be afraid for me. I want this."

"You want it *now*, bright eyes. You may not want it later, when reality sets in. Some mistakes can never be put right."

She closed her eyes, fighting to still the tremors within her body. "This doesn't feel wrong. Does it feel wrong to you?"

"Jamie . . ." He kissed her warm, swollen mouth. "It doesn't matter what I feel. You've been through too much too fast. You need time to heal."

She didn't want this generous gift of time he was giving her. She simply didn't know how to refuse it. He stood slowly, both hands slipping into the pockets of his jeans. There was a moment of quick-breathing silence, when it seemed he was making the decision again, whether to go or stay. Then he smiled faintly, his eyes dark and shuttered.

"Rest now," he said. "We have all the time in the world."

Someone was knocking. Jamie groaned and rolled over on the bed, burying her face in the pillow. She had to be dreaming. No one came knocking in the wilderness.

Then it came again, rousing her to consciousness. Three sharp raps on the screen door. Someone *had* come visiting in the wilderness. Jamie's automatic reflexes took over. Cotton-mouthed, heavy-eyed, she plodded from the bedroom to the living room. It seemed awfully dark. The heavy front door had been left open for ventilation, and a chilly breeze shivered through the room. Casey Fletcher stood behind the screen door, smiling through the wire mesh. Behind him the Wyoming sky had cooled to a frosty violet.

"House call," Casey announced cheerfully. He was wearing a tan buckskin shirt with laces that crisscrossed his chest, threadbare jeans, and brown suede moccasins. His hair was secured at the nape of his neck with a faded red bandanna.

Jamie didn't even blink at his unorthodox appearance. She had decided that Casey Fletcher was a law unto himself. "I've never had a house call before," she said, opening the screen door. "I'm touched."

"You should be," Casey said. He walked into the room with a lazy, catlike grace, his moccasins silent on the hardwood floor. "It's after office hours, you know. This goes to show what a dedicated physician you have." He grinned, his teeth flashing white

117

in the shadows. "Actually, it shows my partiality for good-looking redheads. I had a sorrel mare when was ten. Best damn horse I ever owned."

Jamie smiled, knuckling her sleepy eyes. "I remind you of a horse?"

"Her name was Ginger." He assumed a reverent expression. "I could give you no greater compliment, ma'am. If you knew me better, you would realize that. Aren't we missing someone here? Did Hogan fly off to Miami after all?"

"He was here when I went to bed," Jamie said. *Boy, was he ever.* She stood on tiptoe, catching sight of the red Honda through the screen door. "The car's here. I guess he went for a walk or something." Now that the drug-induced oblivion of sleep had vanished, reality was scurrying in. A flood of memories sent her pulses softly pounding. Chris. The bedroom. The invitation. The rejection. She closed her eyes briefly, a troubled frown cutting between her brows. She had to stop this. The less she thought about this afternoon, the better.

"Is your wrist hurting you?" Casey asked quietly.

"No, it's fine." Actually it gave a fiery little twinge with every beat of her heart, but she wasn't about to take another pain pill.

Better to suffer discomfort than humiliation.

"I have to admit, I didn't expect you to be tucked into bed at six o'clock at night. Did the pain pills I prescribed relax you a little too much?"

Jamie nodded, avoiding his eyes. "You could say that. Would you like to sit down?"

"I would," Casey said, "but it's so dark in here I can't see to find a chair. What say we turn on a few lights? I'd like to take a good look at that wrist."

The cabin was equipped with a generator that provided a rather erratic flow of electricity. While the lamps on either side of the sofa hummed and flickered, Casey removed the Ace bandage and carefully examined Jamie's wrist. His expert touch reaffirmed Jamie's opinion that he was a dedicated physician first and a startling nonconformist second.

"It's looking better," he said finally. He replaced the bandage, humming "She'll Be Comin' Round the Mountain" while he rolled. "There we go. Keep it wrapped up for a couple of days. Have you got enough pain pills?"

"Oh, more than enough."

"Terrific. Well, now my professional responsibilities are out of the way." He

119

smiled, stretched his long legs out before him, and hooked his arms behind his neck. "So! What's for dinner, Ginger?"

"Steaks," Jamie replied promptly, "and don't call me Ginger. Would you like to stay for dinner, Doctor?"

"Love to. Hey, it's mighty cool in here. Why don't I get a fire going?"

"Please do." Jamie pointed at the fireplace with an impish grin. "First in there, and then in the *damn* stove."

"The damn stove?"

"That's what Chris calls it. We've had a little trouble getting the damn stove to work. Paper towels burn beautifully, but wood is another story."

"I'll see what I can do." His warm brown eyes studied her thoughtfully. "Actually, you're much better looking than Ginger. It's really a shame about you and Chris."

Jamie's smile faltered. "What do you mean?"

"It's a shame there *is* a 'you and Chris.'" He sighed deeply and patted her on the shoulder. "Not to worry. My heart's been broken before and I survived. Now pay attention, Ginger. You're about to learn the proper method of laying a fire."

"Don't call me —"

The screen door squealed and slammed.

Chris stood in the doorway, his broad shoulders silhouetted against the dying light. He wore a black sweatshirt, and his cheeks carried the bite of a mountain night. His stance was relaxed, his hooded eyes shining like crystals. He was even smiling, his lips twisted in a sugary curve. "Isn't this nice?" he said. "The little house on the prairie has company."

Jamie felt her heart thudding against her ribs. Chris reminded her of a wildcat ready to spring — waiting, judging. And so still. "Casey dropped by to check on my wrist," she said. She looked from one man to the other. When neither spoke she added brightly, "I've invited him to dinner, on the condition he gets the stove working."

"Sounds fair." Chris kicked the heavy front door closed with his foot. "I hope you have better luck with the damn stove than I've had, Fletcher."

"Wood-burning stoves can be tricky," Casey replied, his tone serene.

Everyone smiled, and no one moved. Jamie endured the deafening silence as long as she could, then stood up abruptly. "I'm freezing in these shorts. Excuse me while I change into something warmer."

"You're excused," Chris said silkily.

She made a beeline for the bedroom and

stayed there as long as possible. Fifteen minutes later, dressed in pink twill slacks and a pink sweater, she poked her head out the bedroom door. An honest-to-goodness fire was alive and well in the fireplace, spreading a warm red glow across the living room. From the kitchen came the husky murmurs of male voices. From this distance, they sounded civil. Not friendly, perhaps, but civil. She could also smell the mouthwatering aroma of sizzling steaks. At this point, Jamie was so hungry she would have entered a war zone to reach those steaks.

Actually, the atmosphere in the kitchen was almost cozy. Casey was sitting at the kitchen table, cutting up lettuce and tomatoes with a hunting knife that Crocodile Dundee would have envied. Chris was standing over the stove, flipping steaks in a frying pan with a pancake turner.

"Hey," Casey said, spotting Jamie in the doorway. "I was beginning to wonder if you'd dozed off again."

"It just takes a while to get dressed with this hand." Jamie wandered into the room, avoiding Chris's eyes. "The steaks smell good."

"I hope you like yours well done." Chris's voice was light and arid. "We've been waiting for you."

Jamie managed an almost-smile. "Well, here I am. What can I do to help?"

"Nothing at all." Chris turned then, hitting her with the full force of his brilliant gaze. "Just sit down and enjoy a most pleasant evening."

The fire was nearly out. Casey Fletcher was long gone. Jamie was sitting cross-legged on the living room floor, thumbing through *Field and Stream*. Chris was on the sofa behind her, cracking his knuckles.

"Do you have to do that?" Jamie muttered.

"Do what?"

"You know what! Crack your knuckles. It's annoying."

"Oh." Chris considered for a moment. "Actually, what I find annoying is sitting in a cabin with a sphinx."

"Are you implying I'm not good company?"

"Oh, you're *wonderful* company . . . as long as Doc Holliday is around. The minute he leaves, you're a clam. You roll up in a little ball on the floor. You read anything and everything to avoid looking at me. You jump halfway to the rafters whenever I move a muscle." He touched the side of her neck and she jerked. "I rest my case."

In some cool, logical corner of her mind, Jamie knew she was capable of handling this situation like an adult. If she chose to, she could calmly apologize for her reckless behavior earlier that afternoon. She could lighten this tense, volatile atmosphere with a little humor and some polite chitchat. She could reestablish their earlier pleasant camaraderie.

If she chose to.

She slapped the magazine down on the floor. "I'm going to bed." *Why are you acting like this, Jamie? Why are you pushing him?* "I don't want to inflict myself on you any further if it's such a strain being with me —"

"You have no idea," he muttered behind her. "I think I liked you better when you were sky-high on Demerol. At least then you said what you felt."

Jamie scrambled to her feet. "I don't need to listen to this."

"No, you don't," he agreed, ominously calm. "You can run away from me."

"Don't flatter yourself." Instinctively Jamie clenched both hands into fists, then gasped as an answering fire shot through her injured wrist.

"You ought to be more careful," Chris said. "You can't be throwing temper tantrums while you're an invalid."

124

"I was not throwing . . ." Jamie paused, took a deep breath, and shook back her hair. "I'm going to sleep," she said tonelessly. "It's getting quite chilly in here. You ought to throw another log on the fire before it goes out. Lord knows you'll never get it started again if it does."

A little smile flickered across Chris's lips. He stood slowly, hooking his thumbs into the waistband of his jeans. "Don't worry about me, sweetheart. I can manage to keep a fire going."

There may have been a double entendre in that statement. Jamie chose to ignore it. "You may be able to keep one going," she said sweetly, "but you sure as hell can't start one. If Casey hadn't come by tonight, we'd be licking peanut butter off our fingers right now."

Softly, "The man wears a ponytail."

"The man can start a simple fire."

"There are other things in life, baby."

"No! Really?" Jamie slapped a thoughtful hand on her cheek. "Well, why don't you tell me some of them, Marlowe? Don't be modest. I really want to know. What can *you* do?"

Firelight shimmered across his face in ribbons of red and violet. His hooded eyes gleamed with unclouded temper. With both hands he lifted Jamie up and physically laid her back against the cushions of the sofa. And then he leaned forward, so close she could see the pulse that throbbed at his temple. He brought his hand to her neck, experienced fingers closing with exquisite gentleness around the velvet-soft skin. His face was a carved mask.

"I've managed to acquire a few talents," he said. "I'm terrific at kicking down doors and yelling *freeze*. I make the driest martini in Miami. I play a mean hand of poker. I can eat, write, and shoot just as well with my left hand as my right . . . and I'm a hell of a shot. I can sleep like a baby through a hurricane. I know every word of *Alice's Restaurant* by heart. I can visit the coroner's office and then stop by McDonald's and enjoy a quarter-pounder. I can say 'I love you,' 'You're under arrest,' and 'You have beautiful lips' in six different languages. And do you know what else I can do, Ace?"

Jamie released an uneven breath. "What?"

"I can live under the same roof with the most beautiful, exciting, desirable, frustrating woman I've ever known, and *I can control myself*. And now if you'll excuse me, I'm going to take another damn walk."

CHAPTER

Six

Thus began what Jamie would later refer to as the Cold War of Clearwater County.

The morning following Casey's house call, Jamie woke up to a cold house and a cold note: *Ace — I had some things to take care of in Clearwater. Don't go far from the cabin.*

There wasn't much chance of Jamie wandering too far from the cabin. She was not enamored of the wilderness. It was full of grass and bushes; and grass and bushes disguised dangerous rabbit holes. She took her paper and pen and settled into the porch swing, far above rabbit territory. Her handwriting was becoming almost legible.

DIARY OF A FUGITIVE
Day Two
My wrist feels better. My spirit is broken. This peace and quiet is going to give me a nervous breakdown. Especially the quiet. Even while Chris is away in Clearwater, I can feel him giving me the silent treatment. Obviously he has a problem with ulcer-ridden journalists who throw themselves at his feet — and other

body parts. I don't blame him.

When Chris returned, he gave Jamie a sugary smile and a care package from Eldon Don's Variety Store. He thought Jamie could use a few things to keep her occupied during her involuntary seclusion. He knew how tiresome bunny-watching could become.

Jamie glanced at him suspiciously, then spread the contents of the paper sack on the kitchen table. It certainly was a varied assortment. A cross-stitch kit that read, IN TIME THIS TOO SHALL PASS. A nice, fat book of crossword puzzles. Three Louis L'Amour paperbacks. A thousand-piece jigsaw puzzle. Four skeins of variegated yarn and a crochet hook.

"How very thoughtful of you," Jamie said. "Do you by any chance know how to crochet?"

"Women know these things," Chris said. Then, "Don't you?"

"I'm sure it will come to me," Jamie replied.

"Fine. Good. I think I'll go for a walk."

DIARY OF A FUGITIVE
Day Three
It's a beautiful morning. I'm back in my porch swing, watching Thumper watch

me. Chris has gone for a walk. My private eye has become a walkaholic. He never goes far, just . . . often. He's getting restless. I don't know why he hasn't left for home. I can't imagine being here without him. A cold war is better than no war at all, Book of Jamie, Chapter One.

Last night Chris spent three hours working on a jigsaw puzzle. I spent three hours watching him. He looks good in firelight.

The writer in Jamie looked over Day Three's entry with some disgust. There was no meat there, nothing *interesting*. Then again, nothing interesting had happened since Chris had taken up walking and given up talking.

She was tired of her porch swing. She was tired of the cabin. She went to her room and changed into stiff jeans and a long-sleeved shirt. Walking clothes, designed to protect against biting, stinging, creeping, and crawling things. It was time to visit the Great Outdoors.

Actually, it was almost pleasant once she got through the knee-high grass surrounding the cabin. Autumn came early to the high country. The leaves were tangled shades of scarlet and yellow. Asparagus —

at least it looked like asparagus — grew wild along a rocky stream not fifty yards from the cabin. Bird song and the sound of trickling water filled the air, a melody that the city girl found almost as soothing as the hum of freeway traffic.

Jamie walked slowly through the dappled sunlight, forcing the troubles and tensions of the past few days to the back of her mind. She wouldn't think about why's and hows. She wouldn't think about beginnings and endings. As a matter of fact, she wouldn't think at all. She could hear her footsteps whispering through the grass. The light breeze brushed a pleasant coolness against her face. And the earth — for the first time in her life, she was aware of the fragrance of the earth . . . rich and moist and clean. The surroundings were too alien for her to feel at home here, but she felt . . . welcome.

She crossed a baby stream by hopping on flat, sun-warmed rocks, then followed a narrow path beneath a canopy of trees, telling herself she wasn't really looking for Chris. She followed the trail onward and upward until she ducked through a furry stand of pines and found herself at the crest of a hill. She looked down on a gently sloping meadow, brilliantly colored with a yellow haze of daisies and sunlight. And at the bottom of that meadow, a lone private eye stood knee-deep in daisies, carefully lining up an assortment of Styrofoam cups, aluminum cans, and broken beer bottles on a sagging wooden fence. Apparently a little bit of civilization could be found even here.

Jamie took two steps backward, into the dark shade of the pines. Even from this distance, she could see the breeze picking at his hair, finding the delicate golden highlights. He wore his yellow shirt hanging over his jeans, freshly washed but atrociously wrinkled. He was frowning, as if this challenge of balancing litter on wooden railings required all of his concentration. Jamie was completely bewildered.

Suddenly Chris seemed satisfied with his fence decorating. He turned and walked the full length of the meadow, putting at least seventy-five feet between himself and the fence before he stopped. His back was to the fence, his arms loosely at his sides, his stance easy and relaxed. Watching him, Jamie had a vague memory of an old western she had once seen. Didn't Gary Cooper stand just like that in the split second before he —

Chris suddenly whirled, arms extended, knees slightly bent, a shiny, snub-nosed revolver appearing from nowhere in his hand.

He fired in rapid succession, picking off each and every target on the fence before Jamie could blink. One minute they were there, the next they were gone. The meadow settled into forgiving silence; Chris's arms dropped slowly to his side.

And then . . . and then he repeated the entire exercise this time holding the gun in his left hand.

Jamie discovered her hand was over her mouth. Probably to stifle a startled yelp, she thought. She had no idea her private eye could shoot like that. She had no idea *anyone* could shoot like that, including Gary Cooper.

Chris suddenly turned his head, smiling at her across a field of flowers. He'd known she was there, Jamie realized. He'd known all along.

She picked her way slowly down the hill, keeping a wary eye out for rabbit holes and slithery things. Chris waited at the bottom, hands pushed into the back pockets of his jeans.

When she was close enough to see the sunburn scratching his cheeks, she said curiously, "Where is it?"

He tilted his head, squinting against the sunlight. "Where is what, Ace?"

"You know what," Jamie replied, exasperated. "Your gun. One second you're tripping through the daisies, the next you're armed and dangerous. Where is it?"

He patted a bulge on his shirt. "Here. Shoulder holster."

"Where did it come from? I didn't know you even brought your gun. How did you get it through airport security? Where have you been keeping it? Where did you learn to *shoot* like that?"

Chris raised his eyes to heaven. "Did anyone ever tell you that you have an unnatural obsession with firearms?"

"Healthy curiosity," she said.

Smiling faintly, he plucked a flower from the daisy carpet and worked it into her hair. "Your mother should have expanded on that," he said softly. "Curiosity isn't always healthy, lady bright. There are times when it can be dangerous."

Jamie returned his smile, feeling the nearness of his body tickle hers. "Possibly she should have mentioned that. So . . . are you going to tell me?"

"About the gun?" He sighed, "Let's see, what were the questions? The gun came from my underwear drawer at home. I got it through airport security with a special pass. I've been keeping it on me or near me since the day we left."

"You left one out," Jamie said. "Where did you learn to shoot like that?"

There was an almost imperceptible pause that made her look sharply at him, but she could see nothing unusual in his expression.

"I was a cop for eleven years," he said. "The city of Miami has a way of inspiring a policeman to hit what he aims at. Would you like to learn?"

She blinked sunlight off her lashes. "Learn what?"

"To shoot," he said. "How about some target practice?"

"My wrist."

"Oh, you can hold the gun in your left hand. Believe me, it won't make any difference."

Jamie chose to ignore that comment. She helped him set up another row of cans and bottles on the fence. She walked with him a mere twenty feet across the meadow before he stopped.

"This will do," he said.

"But you shot from clear over —"

"This will do," he said, silencing her with a look. He positioned himself behind Jamie and reached around her, lifting her arms. "There, like that. No, hold your right hand beneath your left wrist to support it. That's it." He put the gun in her hand, his fingers closing around hers, pointing it in the general direction of the fence. "The safety's off, so all you have to do is pull the trigger."

"What about aiming?" Jamie asked, dry-mouthed. He was so close, every breath she took held the fragrance of flowers and heat and man.

"You should aim," he said. "It's always a good idea to aim."

She didn't really like the feel of the gun in her hand. It was cold and hard and heavy, and she couldn't help wondering about the times he had used it for more than target practice. She much preferred the feel of the man behind her, the whisper of his breath stirring her hair, the powerful thighs cradling her hips. Her head told her to concentrate on the targets lined up on the fence. Her body argued gently, insistently, for another target. Keeping the gun pointed somewhere in the vicinity of the fence, Jamie turned her head, looking over her shoulder at Chris. They bumped noses.

"Is this good?" she asked huskily.

His dark lashes blinked once. When he spoke, his voice was a shade deeper than usual. "The gun. Of course you mean the gun. Yes, you're doing fine."

"I've never done this before." If she stood on her toes, she could brush her lips against his. Oh, it was tempting. Especially when his mouth parted just the tiniest bit, looking so soft and vulnerable. Just the way it looked now . . .

Chris cleared his throat. "Look down the nuzzle . . . uh, *muzzle*." His gaze was wandering, from her sun-filled eyes to her freckled nose, from her nose to her lovely, lovely mouth. It took an extraordinary amount of concentration to remember what he intended to say next. "Now you'll need to get a bead on your target." He took a deep breath, trying and failing to control the desire that spiraled through him. No, it was more than desire. Physical need he could control. The emotional need that flared within him was something else altogether, something . . . more.

"I can't do this," he whispered suddenly. "I can't be so close to you and not . . ."

Jamie rose up on tiptoes. "And not . . ."

"Get closer." He lowered his head fractionally, his lips dragging across hers, stroking the warm softness. Drowsy kisses of languidly altering pressure wrung a soft groan from deep in her throat, as she parted her lips for a deeper, hungrier assault. The isolation and the uncertainty of the preceding days burned away under his desperate, yearning touch. Nothing existed in the world but his need to bring her close, closer . . .

The gun suddenly fired. It wasn't something one could ignore, even while in the throes of mindless passion. Jamie nearly jumped out of her skin, staggering slightly, breaking the kiss with a gasp and a yelp. Her head swiveled, she stared at the bottles and cans on the fence. There had been six targets before, now there were five.

"I hit something," she said breathlessly. "I don't believe this. I actually *hit* something."

"It's a miracle." Hands on her shoulders, he turned her to face him. Gently he took the gun from her fingers, clicked on the safety, and slipped it into the holster beneath his shirt. Looking into her sparkling eyes he felt a smile start way down inside him, like a tickle. The sun was hot on his shoulders and back. The air was filled with flowers and sweet anticipation. The day was young and rich with possibilities.

He'd never felt so happy in his life.

His smile stretched. It softened his eyes and warmed his chest. It pushed at his cheeks until they ached, and he was absurdly pleased to see her smile grow right along with his. And then suddenly they both were laughing, holding on to each other for support, heads thrown back in the bright, sun-washed air. They were laughing as though they didn't know how to stop, as though they had grown tired of trying to find logic in the peculiar universe they created together.

When he found his voice, Chris said again, "It's a miracle, Jamie Cross."

Jamie only nodded, blinking away pleasure tears. She didn't say anything. For once in her life, words were totally inadequate to describe her thoughts and feelings. She didn't want to try. Looking at Chris, she realized she didn't need to try.

"Do you like parades?" Chris asked suddenly.

Did she like parades? Still trembling from laughter and desire, Jamie had to think a minute before answering. "Yes. I like parades."

"And peaches?"

"Yes," she said dazedly. "Peaches, too. Is there a reason you're asking me this —"

"You'll need to change," he said. "One of those nice pink dresses I bought for you would be good."

"Good for *what?*"

"Nosy, aren't you?" His eyes twinkled as he bent to kiss her nose. "No more questions. You have to learn to trust me, Ace.

Put yourself totally in my hands. Follow my instructions unconditionally. Have blind faith in my judgment —"

"You're pushing it."

"Okay. I'll settle for the benefit of the doubt." He was still laughing with his eyes. His hands were on her shoulders, performing a gentle, mesmerizing massage. "Will you spend the day with me, Jamie?"

"I won't wear pink," she said.

She wore pink.

Actually she wore pink and white — a candy-cane striped top and a white denim skirt. Her hair was tied loosely on top of her head with white embroidery floss from her cross-stitch kit. One made do in the wilderness.

"I don't ordinarily dress like this," Jamie said, watching the shaggy green trees zipping past the car window. "It would kill my credibility to investigate a story in a white miniskirt."

Chris smiled, gearing down to negotiate a hairpin curve. "Oh, I can see it now. All those career woman clothes you have — excuse me, *had* — in your closet at home. Lots of sensible suits with little shoulder pads. White button-down shirts. Go-anywhere dresses that don't need to be ironed. Comfortable jeans and baggy T-shirts for those midnight marathons with your computer."

He was awfully close to the truth, but Jamie could see no reason to admit it. "Better to look like a career woman," she said sweetly, "than a bimbo. Your taste runs to the short, tight, and transparent, Marlowe."

"I resent that," he said mildly. "I put a lot of thought into those clothes. Eighteen minutes worth."

Jamie tipped her head back on the seat, absorbed in the wild and rugged scenery around them. She tried to put a name to the sweet lassitude filling her soul. Neurotic nail-biter that she was, it took a minute to identify the feeling: pure and simple relaxation. Even a white miniskirt couldn't faze her lovely tranquility.

She glanced sideways at her private eye. He had changed into a white knit shirt that set off the sunburned darkness of his skin. He caught her eye and smiled faintly, that bewitching, adorably boyish smile that turned her bones to honey. He might be able to shoot like Gary Cooper but he had the smile of an innocent Boy Scout. How very misleading, Jamie thought, remembering the erotic demand those lips had made on her, the way he had tasted and felt and smelled. The memories warmed her like a sunshower. She discovered that her newfound tranquility in no way dulled her to the silent, sexual undertones shivering between them. Or perhaps, in some strange way, one was a natural result of the other.

It was probably a good idea to keep the conversation moving along, before she gave in to the desire to throw her very relaxed body across the gearshift and drown him in kisses. These mountain roads were dangerous enough.

"I'm curious about something," she said.

"Darling woman, I would think you were deathly ill if you *weren't* curious about something. However" — he slanted a warning brow in her direction — "if you're going to ask me what I have planned for today, save your breath. It's a surprise."

"No, it's not that." Absently she tugged at the miniskirt, trying to lengthen it an inch or two. "After watching your target practice this morning, I'm more confused than ever. You're an expert shot. You're unbelievably calm under pressure. Everything I know about you tells me you were probably an exceptional cop. I can't understand why you would resign after eleven years."

Chris was silent for so long she thought he

wasn't going to answer at all. Then he said quietly, "It's complicated. I realized I was better suited to another line of work."

Jamie frowned, thinking of his disparaging remarks about the life of a private investigator. As she looked up with a question on her lips, she saw the expression on his face and hesitated. He looked shaken, as if she'd taken him completely by surprise, taken him into memories that were far from pleasant. And his eyes . . . his eyes had darkened to a shrouded, misty gray, hiding far more than they revealed. If eyes were the mirrors of the soul, what secrets could lay in the depths of Chris Hogan's?

And there in the little red car, surrounded by unrelenting greenery and monster mountains, Jamie had a revelation. She had no idea if she would ever understand this man, but she knew she was committed to trying.

She loved him.

Eyes wide, she turned her head slowly to the window. Well. Love had come only once before in her short life, and it had been as breathtaking and short-lived as the glitter of fading fireworks. When the passion died, there were two strangers left tiptoeing around one another, frustrated and helpless to resurrect that desperate need. This feeling was something quite different, something stronger and far more powerful. She wanted to give him things, the very best things. She wanted to know his mind as well as his body. And she wanted to protect him from his sorrows.

"Something happened to you," she said, still staring out the window. "I wish you could tell me. Sometimes it helps to share things."

Flatly, "It's not my way." Then he shook back his hair, found a teasing smile, and took his hand off the gearshift long enough to tug at her ponytail. "No long faces today, Ace. It's not allowed. Today belongs to peaches and sunshine and parades."

"I wish you would tell me where on earth we're —"

"Look! A road pancake. Name that animal in three guesses."

Jamie covered her face with her hands. "I can't take this. I'm a delicate city girl. Give me muggers and street gangs and choking smog, nice familiar things." She peeked through her fingers, watching the familiar WELCOME TO CLEARWATER sign slide by. "We're going to a parade in Clearwater?"

"You've been to Macy's Thanksgiving Parade?" Chris asked.

"Yes."

"Did you have a good time?"

She gave him a suddenly amused look. "Of course I had a good time. I was twelve years old. I thought it was fantastic."

"Then you're in for a real treat, city girl. I have it on the best authority that Macy's Thanksgiving Day Parade is peanuts compared to the Peach Days Parade in Clearwater, Wyoming."

CHAPTER

Seven

Macy's Thanksgiving Day Parade it wasn't. And yet Jamie couldn't remember a day in her life when she had enjoyed herself more.

First there were the floats. Jamie and Chris sat on the sidewalk curb in front of Eldon Don's Variety Store and clapped and cheered for each one that rolled by. The 4-H float decorated with crepe-paper flowers and papier-mâché fruits and vegetables. The Chamber of Commerce float, proudly displaying a twelve-foot-high plaster replica of the Grand Tetons. The royalty float bearing a buxom Miss Peach Days and her two pink-cheeked attendants. Chris clapped especially loudly for the royalty float. Watching him, watching his smile and the silky-soft hair tumbling in the breeze, Jamie could hardly believe he was a day over seventeen. Totally content, she would drink him in with her eyes until he squirmed under her thoughtful regard. And then he would kiss her on the cheek and ask her to please watch the parade. Fascinated and delighted with his gruff self-consciousness, Jamie felt the last of her defenses slipping away like sand through her fingers. The man was a miracle, with his sad-sweet eyes and bone-melting smile, and he had no idea.

There was a marching band from the local high school, complete with miniskirted baton twirlers wearing outfits quite similar to Jamie's. An honorary sheriff's posse mounted on gleaming palominos trotted by, waving spotless white cowboy hats at the crowd. A cherry-red convertible idled along, bearing the officers of Clearwater High's graduating class of 1949. Jamie cheered until she was hoarse, feeling more at home than she had in days. This happy confusion was a blessed thing to behold. Jamie had always thrived on confusion.

Afterward they followed the crowds around the block to the Clearwater Municipal Park. There, scattered out over two baseball diamonds, an entire western carnival was taking place. There was a merry-go-round, pony rides, fortune tellers, a chuck-wagon lunch, midway games, and a miniature Ferris wheel. Food was plentiful, most of it promoting the honored peach. There were peach snow cones, peach pies, frozen peach yogurt, and homemade peach ice cream. There were also bushels and bushels of fresh peaches for sale, filling the air with a sweet, mouth-watering fragrance. Jamie bought a half-bushel herself, leaving it beneath the shade of a giant sycamore while they played. She didn't worry about it being stolen. There was something about this sunny, happy-go-lucky atmosphere that made such a thing seem impossible.

They rode on the Ferris wheel four times. The power went off once briefly, leaving them swinging in their little metal bucket at the top of the sky. Jamie was startled into dropping her cotton candy. Wondering what and who it might have hit, she leaned over the bar so far that Chris had to clamp his hand on her shoulder and drag her back.

"You terrify me," he said. His tawny, flyaway hair was falling around his face and his eyes were the color of the hot summer sky. "Think before you jump, sweet thing."

Jamie grinned, licking the sticky, sugary candy off her lips. "Nah. That takes the excitement out of living. I like spontaneity."

"Dropping out of a Ferris wheel is certainly spontaneous." He couldn't take his hands off her for fear she would fall. He couldn't take his eyes off her for fear she would disappear. She was the most beautiful thing he had ever seen in his life. Her shirt was stained with peach juice. Her hair was escaping from the ponytail, falling in silky tendrils on her sunburned neck. Her eyes were filled with sunlight and laughter and focused with sweet intensity on her private eye ninety-nine percent of the time. He had no idea what she saw when she looked at him. He only hoped that by some miracle she found what she was searching for.

"You're staring," Jamie said huskily.

Chris nodded slowly. "Yeah, I know."

"Do I have food on my face or something?"

"Uh-huh." He sighed, dipping his forehead against hers, rubbing in a gentle, circular motion. His fingers touched her lips. "You have sugar . . . there."

Jamie's eyes were softly unfocused as she gazed at his mouth. "Where?"

"Here . . ." His tongue slipped across the corner of her mouth, and her lips parted on a sigh, savoring the fiery warmth of his caress as he gently touched, tasted, and then pulled away. It wasn't a kiss — it was the most erotic promise she had ever been given.

Jamie took a ragged, unsatisfying breath. "Oh boy," she said eloquently.

Chris threaded his fingers slowly through hers. His eyes were dark and solemn. "Jamie," he said softly, "I want you to know that . . ."

She waited, her breath fluttering and dying in her throat. "What?"

He hesitated, then shook his head, a wry smile curling his lips. "Never mind. It's not the time."

The uncertainty in his voice caught Jamie by the heart. She saw his vulnerability only in glimpses, but the conviction grew within her that this strong man needed her — needed her as desperately as she needed him.

They had time, she told herself. They had all the time they needed to find their way.

Holding hands, they wandered through the bright whirl of carnival music and jovial confusion in the park. They ate dripping barbecued beef sandwiches and sweet corn on the cob for dinner. Jamie noticed that the sun had been replaced by gaily blinking lights strung across the night sky. A blue-grass band was playing on a makeshift stage in the center of the park. They followed the music, crowding shoulder to shoulder with the swaying, clapping audience. After a particularly rousing song, Jamie startled Chris with her remarkable ability to give an ear-piercing whistle through her front teeth. He clapped a hand over her mouth and told her to behave.

They were digging into their third bag of

popcorn that day when Casey Fletcher strolled across their path. True to the spirit of the celebration, his hair was braided and tied with a peach-colored ribbon. Other than that, his clothing was unusually conservative — white jeans and a raspberry-colored T-shirt.

"My favorite patient," he said cheerfully, his observant gaze taking in the hectic flush on Jamie's cheeks and the food stains on her shirt. "You look like you're having a good time. How are you, Hogan?"

"Fine, thanks," Chris said. The two men shook hands, polite but less than enthusiastic. "You were right. This was just the thing to lift Jamie's spirits." Then, to Jamie, "I met Casey in town yesterday. He's the one who told me about the Peach Days celebration."

"Then I owe you one, Doctor," Jamie said to Casey. "I've never had more fun in my life."

"I specialize in fun," Casey replied, "and don't call me doctor." He grabbed a handful of popcorn from the bag Jamie was holding and threw it into his mouth. "Well, I hate to eat and run, but duty calls. The merry-go-round proved too much for poor Mrs. Delahunt."

Jamie's eyes stretched. "She was hurt?"

"Nope." His eyes sparkled with dark humor. "She's nine months pregnant. There was something about the horses going up and down and the carousel going round and round that set her off. The pains are five minutes apart. Catch you later, guys. Oh, and don't tell anyone I specialize in fun. Mrs. Delahunt thinks I specialize in obstetrics."

Smiling, Jamie watched him wander off into the bright confusion of the crowd. "A strange man," she said. "The world should have more strange men like him."

"You're right." Chris's tone was oddly subdued, a cynical spark lighting his eyes. "He's perfectly happy with his life. He is what he wants to be, he's doing what he wants to do. Not everyone can manage that."

Jamie's expression changed, and she touched his arm with her hand, lightly, questioningly. "Is it so hard to be what you want to be?"

The smile he turned on her was less than reassuring. "Not so hard," he said softly. "Just too late."

Jamie shook her head almost violently. "You don't mean that. I know you. You're good and strong and gentle. You give so much more than you take. How can you be

151

unhappy with that?"

"Never mind." Chris was amazed at how close he had come to confiding in her. You could bleed to death opening old wounds, particularly deep ones. He wanted no hint of sadness touching this day. The circle of hurt had to stop. Looking at Jamie, he knew that another circle had begun, a circle of love and friendship and hope. He had to concentrate on that. He had to make it work. He found his very best and brightest smile and sent it flashing in her direction. "I didn't mean to rain on your parade, Ace. I get morbid when I eat too much popcorn. Forgive me."

"There's nothing to forgive." So he wanted to curl up behind his sweet smile and pretend he'd given nothing away. Jamie didn't know what else to do but go along with him for the time being. She understood without words how important it was to Chris that he make her happy today. "So tell me," she said slowly, "do you feel like living dangerously today, Marlowe?"

His blue eyes narrowed suspiciously. "What do you have in mind?"

"The merry-go-round." She took his hand, laughing and dragging him through the crowd. "It must be some ride if it can send poor Mrs. Delahunt into labor. I'd never forgive myself if I didn't give it a try."

Jamie sat on a plaster camel with two humps and a toothy grin. Chris rode a white stallion with a shiny red saddle. Jamie's camel went up and down, Chris's horse went back and forth. As the carousel turned, they became the center of the universe, a musical, magical whirl of color and sound in the darkness of night. The spectators became a blur as the carousel picked up speed. Jamie giggled and focused on Chris to keep her stomach firmly in place. "I'm beginning to feel for Mrs. Delahunt," she said, raising her voice to be heard above the music. "This was a lot more fun when I was six years old."

Chris smiled at the picture she made — the best-known journalist in Miami riding a yellow camel, her ponytail bouncing behind. "You look about six years old," he said. And she was so beautiful, with the deep color staining her cheeks and the soiled bandage padding her wrist and the angel's smile curving her cherry-red lips. Too many snow cones, he thought. Her lips were probably stained forever.

Quietly, so quietly he could barely hear himself above the music, he said, "I think I love you."

But Jamie heard him. She would have

heard him if he'd been swinging from the top of the Ferris wheel. She stared at him. Tenderness and desire flooded her like warm honey poured on her skin. Her pulse beat hard in her throat. She beckoned him with a crooked finger.

Chris tried to kiss her as they rode. It was impossible. His horse went forward when her camel went up. He vaulted off his uncooperative steed, impatient and determined and happier than he'd ever imagined being. One hand curved around the candy-striped post that Jamie clung to, the other lifted her chin with barely restrained urgency. He kissed her cheek, her forehead, and then found her mouth in a long, soul-stirring kiss that lasted until the music died and the carousel stopped turning. He lifted his head slowly, his breath coming in hard shocks. When he spoke, his voice was a hoarse whisper. "Being with you, loving you . . . is the sweetest thing . . ."

"You love me." It wasn't a question. It was a shaky prayer of thanks.

He smiled, looking breathtakingly young with his windblown hair and his heart in his eyes. "I think I've loved you since I saw your pretty little face staring at me from a jail cell. It was an unforgettable moment."

"Oh, don't remind me." She touched the

heat in his cheeks with trembling fingers. "Did I happen to mention that —"

"Oh, no." The carousel was starting again. The last thing that Chris wanted at this point was another carousel ride. Putting both hands on Jamie's waist, he lifted her up and off her camel. "It's time to go."

She smiled, jumping off the merry-go-round and into his arms. "Where to? The midway games? The Ferris wheel again?"

"Actually . . ." He pulled her close, light kindling in his eyes as he studied her face. "I kind of thought we'd go home."

"I kind of like that idea," Jamie whispered.

The ride home was unusually quiet. Chris seemed absorbed in his thoughts. Jamie's heartbeat was jumping, jumping. She stared at him shamelessly. He was beautiful. His lazy, gemstone eyes were tucked at the corners with a forgotten smile. His cheekbones were shadowed with a hard flush and the breeze from the open window moved restlessly through his hair. He gave the impression of being completely relaxed in an extremely tense sort of way . . . if such a thing were possible.

They were too far apart, Jamie decided. She unbuckled her seatbelt and maneuvered her way into touching distance. She smoothed the hair back from his brow and smiled when the wind tumbled it forward again. She pressed a whisper-light kiss on his neck, then another. The muscles beneath her lips seemed to tighten.

"*Not* a good idea," Chris muttered, staring straight ahead.

She sighed, resting her chin on his shoulder. "It's a long ride and you seemed so far away."

"I'm with you in spirit, believe me."

"Would you like me to go back to my side of the car?"

His eyes gleamed in the soft light from the instrument panel. "Yeah . . . in a minute."

She was still nestled against him when they pulled up in front of the cabin twenty minutes later. He killed the engine and the headlights, then turned to her in a companionable gesture. "I suppose," he mused thoughtfully, "we should decide where to go from here."

Jamie looked at the cabin, then back at Chris. "You don't know?"

"Well, we've got a couple of options." He tugged gently on the white embroidery floss in her hair, watching the silky copper strands tumbling to her shoulders. "We could go for a walk. There's a full moon tonight."

Was he serious? Jamie had walked more today than she had in the past year. "Any other options?"

"Sure. We could go inside and work on the jigsaw puzzle and break open a package of Fig Newtons. It's entirely up to you. A romantic walk in the moonlight or a challenging jigsaw puzzle. Either one is fine with me, really."

Slowly Jamie found her own seat again. Was he teasing? Nervous? Having second thoughts? Trying to take it slow for her sake?

"Are you?" she asked baldly.

Chris smiled, twirling the embroidery floss around his index finger. "Am I what?"

"Teasing, nervous, having second thoughts, or trying to take it slow for my sake?"

"I guess I forgot to tell you the third option. We could also go into the cabin, light a fire — if you know what's good for you, you won't laugh — and I could give up my death grip on my self-control. While you think about it, I'll pray."

Jamie didn't need to think about it. She opened her car door, then, liberated lady that she was, she walked around and opened his. Taking him by the hand, she walked slowly through the grass and up the creaking wooden steps to the front door. It was locked. Her private eye was ever so vigilant.

"I'll unlock it," Chris said, the faintest tremor underscoring his deep voice. And he tried, but it took him a full thirty seconds before he realized he was using the car key. Mouth tightening, he switched to the proper key on his key ring. "Don't laugh, please," he said, throwing the door wide. "I've never done this before."

Jamie took two steps into the cabin, then swung around to face him as his words sunk in. "What did you say?"

"I said I've never done this before." He stepped inside and closed the door behind him. His eyes were a fiery network of colors in the darkness, burning where they touched. "Not with someone I loved," he said softly.

Jamie had to remind herself to breathe. Suddenly it all became so very, very serious. "You could break my heart," she whispered.

He walked toward her, his footsteps echoing on the wooden floor. "And you could break mine."

Her hand found his face in the shadows, touching the strong, square jaw, the sandpaper beard, the softly parted lips. "I need you, Chris. I don't know what's going to happen to me tomorrow or next week or next year . . . but I'd choose a broken heart over never knowing what it would be like to be with you. I think that's the one thing I couldn't face."

"Nothing's going to happen to you, Jamie." He took her face in his hands, his thumbs sculpting the hollows beneath her cheekbones. "With God as my witness, I swear to you that only good things are going to come to you, that you're only going to know happiness and love."

"You can't make that promise," Jamie said. "No one knows what tomorrow will bring. You can't give me immunity from life. I wouldn't want it if you could." She moved closer, her body arching against his, her hands yearning over his chest. "But you can give me love. You can fill me with so much love that I'll be able to face anything the future holds."

"I'm so lost in you," Chris whispered. Slowly his smile came back, the gentle, boyish smile she so loved. "There's nothing and no one in the world for me but you. I can't think, Jamie. I can't seem to do anything but just . . . feel . . ." He bent his head, nuzzling the feverish skin of her throat, then moving his lips lower. His hands slipped over her breasts, pressing and kneading. "So soft . . ."

They forgot about the fire. They forgot about the darkness. They came together with a sudden fierce need, wanting more than the mating of tongues and lips. Jamie pressed into him. He pulled her even closer. Her hands pulled urgently at his shirt, until he stopped holding her long enough to tug it over his head and toss it on the floor. If there was a more graceful way of undressing when your body was on fire and your mind was unraveling, Chris didn't know it.

Jamie's hand was at the waistband of her skirt. Chris stopped her, saying huskily, "No. Let me. I've dreamed about this, and wished . . ."

Jamie guided his hand to the zipper at her side. The only light in the room came from his eyes, drawing her gaze like a crackling fire. Staring at him, she felt her skirt slip to the floor. She stepped out of the skirt and her sandals and back into his arms. "I'm cold," she said. "Keep me warm."

She rode in his arms into the silent shadows of the bedroom. Her pink and white knit top was left somewhere in the hall. They tumbled together on the bed, his jeans scratching her long bare legs, his hands moving hungrily over the pale lace that covered her breasts. Eager and artless, they kissed until kissing was more of a torture than a salve. His hands stroked the delicate hollow of her back, kneaded her buttocks, slipped beneath the silky underpants to pull her even closer. Jamie was shuddering, painfully aware of a gnawing emptiness inside her that begged to be filled.

"Wait," he whispered, when her hands worked feverishly at his belt buckle. He stood up, shrugging out of his clothes and kicking them aside. And then when Jamie held out her hands to him, he shook his head. "No," he said. "I want to see you." He turned on the lamp beside the bed, flooding a very small corner of the room with a very soft light. "Come here, Jamie."

Her legs felt shaky and unreliable, but she managed the two steps it took her to reach him and his halo of light. He looked down at her for the longest time, just looked at her. He wanted to hold on to this moment almost as badly as he wanted to touch her. Her hair was a wild, soft tangle around her face and shoulders. Her lips were swollen and tender. Her eyes had taken on a sleepy sensuality he could feel in the lower part of his body.

"I love you," he said.

Jamie's smile was unsteady. Holding his eyes, she lifted her silk camisole up and over her head. Slippery light smoothed over her body, revealing the supple moist skin of her breasts. She heard the sharp intake of his breath and her smile grew stronger. She slipped her panties over her hips, dropping them to the floor.

"You're going to be the death of me," Chris said hoarsely, "and I'm looking forward to it."

His head bent to her dusky nipple and Jamie's stomach convulsed in a hard reflex. The gentle biting, suckling motions his mouth made left her weak and shivering. She couldn't stand. He lowered her to the bed, dragging her into a deep kiss that soon turned frantic. He kissed every part of her, leading her into a reckless delirium of pleasure. His own eyes were softly blurred as he spoke to her in hoarse, half-formed thoughts and husky endearments. "I didn't know . . . sweet love . . . you feel so good. I want to bury myself in you . . . die in you . . ."

He held her hips steady, entering her by sighs and inches. So slowly . . . lost in her eyes, lost in the warmth and softness and heat of her. He wanted to tell her, to find the words that would let her know how desperately he needed her. But he'd never been good with words, and the frustration burned his throat.

"I know," Jamie whispered, reading the silent message in his eyes. "Oh, Chris . . . I know." She wrapped her legs around him, savoring the agonizing pleasure of finally being joined together. She wanted to go on and she wanted to stay where she was. Then Chris began a rhythm that set her on fire. Ecstasy surrounded them, burning their senses, taking them into a sweet violence that was beyond control. Jamie repeated his name over and over, asking him to help her, to hold her . . .

Chris was burning up, feverish. The need was building and the yearning was too much to endure. She was killing him softly, dragging his spirit to a place he had never been before. He hadn't thought himself capable of such intense emotional and physical sharing. They were on the carousel again, spinning into space, faster and faster until they knew nothing beyond shared rapture. And together they found a release so piercingly sweet, so exquisitely painful, that it was both a welcome death and a dazzling birth.

CHAPTER

Eight

Jamie knew he was gone before she opened her eyes. The bed was cold. Her arms felt empty.

It took her a few minutes to adjust to consciousness and darkness and loneliness all at once. She raised up on her elbow, blinking in the shadows until a dark figure standing near the window came into focus.

"What are you doing?" she asked, her voice thick with sleep.

His head turned slightly. She could barely make out the outline of his profile. "Go back to sleep, Jamie," he said quietly. "Everything's fine."

"How can you say that? I'm here and you're way over there." She turned on the lamp near her bed, sheltering her eyes against the sudden light. "Did you hear something? Is someone out there?"

"There's no one out there." His voice was soothing, as if he were talking to a child after an unsettling dream. "I told you, everything's fine. Go back to sleep."

Everything was not fine. Instinctively Jamie knew he was a world away from her.

She pulled a sheet off the bed and huddled inside it, more as a concession to the chill air than to modesty. The floor was cold, cold, cold. She danced over to him, making breathless suffering noises. She had goosebumps on goosebumps. How could Chris stand there dressed in nothing but a pair of jeans — unzipped, at that — and talk without his teeth chattering?

"This is true devotion," Jamie said. "Small people like yours truly freeze to death very quickly. Why are you looking out the window?"

"I like to watch the sunrise." Even his voice seemed far away.

"It's still pitch black out there."

Softly, "You can see the outline of the mountains. It won't be long."

Something was so very wrong. Something more than sleeplessness or a desire to watch the sunrise. Jamie touched his cheek with cold fingers. "Talk to me. Please talk to me."

There was a moment of silence. Then he pulled her gently in front of him, her hips cradled in the warmth of his body. He rested his chin on her shoulder, and his strong brown arms circled her waist. "Better?" he whispered.

"Yes." Jamie sighed, settling naturally

into his embrace. There was something about this atmosphere — the cold, the isolation, the unrelenting darkness — that made their shrouded intimacy all the more potent.

"I love it here." Chris's voice was dreamy and intense. "It's so peaceful . . . so quiet. I've decided this is real civilization."

"Is it?" Jamie stared at the dark curtain beyond the window. "If this is civilization, what's waiting for us in Miami?"

"I'm not sure." While he had held Jamie in his arms earlier, his grip on the present and the future had been strong. He loved and was loved, and reality was the miracle they created together. Then all too soon it was over, and he discovered he still faced the gnawing uncertainty inside that physical satisfaction couldn't fill. To try and hold on to anything in this moment-by-moment world was to try and hold back the sunrise. There was a time when the razor-sharp edge between what was and what might be had fascinated him. A risk had been nothing more than a challenge, and Lady Luck had always been on his side.

No. Not always.

He was so still. Jamie shivered, though not from the cold. She could feel him leave her again just as surely as if he'd walked out the door. Her hands closed over his wrists at her waist. "I've asked you before. I'm asking you again. Tell me what it is that has such a hold on you. Let me share it."

"Ancient history, Jamie."

"I don't think so," she said softly. "You're keeping it alive."

He turned her slowly into his arms. His eyes were as shadowed and mysterious as the night around them. "Sweet love . . . I appreciate your concern, but it isn't necessary. You've made me happier than I've ever been in my life. Don't you know that?"

Jamie's hands slipped around his neck. The sheet fell to the floor. "Someday you'll tell me," she whispered, "but for now I suppose I'll just have to be content with making you happier than you've ever been in your life."

His smile shimmered through the darkness. "Dirty job, but you're the only one who can do it. You're trembling, madam. I think you're a little underdressed for the mountain night."

"I think you're right." Her breasts brushed against his chest and her stomach molded to his. "I need something warm and heavy on top of me. Any suggestions?"

"Lady, have I got a suggestion for you . . ."

Much later, when the sunlight was

slanting through the window and the heat was building in the little room, Chris stretched out on the tumbled bedcovers, staring down at the ravished angel beside him. "This must be what paradise is like," he said softly.

"Paradise?" Jamie smiled crookedly, glancing around their rustic surroundings. "Are you sure about that?"

He looked at her, and deep within the steel-blue eyes was a light of gratitude and wonder. "It's the closest I've come for a long, long time."

DIARY OF A FUGITIVE
Days Four, Five, and Six

All right, so I've been a little lax in writing. I've also been very busy. There are a multitude of things to do with your lover in the wilderness. No, scratch that. There are a multitude of things to do in the wilderness when you're with your lover. Better.

We're heavily into picnicking. We also do a lot of rabbit watching and bird watching and target shooting. In the evenings we sit around the old jigsaw puzzle. Every rustic pastime is absolutely fascinating when you're totally preoccupied with what you're going to do after you finish doing whatever it is you're doing at the moment. Oh my. I need to go back to work. I'm losing my ability to express myself.

And speaking of work . . . I've managed a few quiet moments to work up another piece on Miselli. I think it's the best thing I've ever done. I feel invigorated again, ready to do battle. Ain't love grand?

Day Seven commenced with a downpour that thrashed the trees and packed the bushes flat to the ground. By noon the skies were partly cloudy and the steam was rising from the earth in wispy spirals.

"Perfect walking weather," Chris said, pulling on a hooded black sweatshirt he found in a closet. "Let's go."

"Why don't you go without me?" Jamie was yawning between every other word. Her nights had been far more active of late, and she was in need of a nice nap. "I'm tired. I think I'd rather curl up with a friendly pillow."

Chris pulled her off the sofa and thrust a huge green windbreaker into her hands. "Here. It's a little big, but it's all I could find. At least you'll stay dry."

"Maybe you didn't hear me." She gave the windbreaker back. "I'm going to take a nap."

169

"You need exercise." The windbreaker changed hands again. "Put a little color in your cheeks. You've been spending way too much time in bed lately."

"I love you. I need you. I desire you and admire you, but I do not want to take a walk with you."

"All right." He plopped down on the sofa, propping his legs on the coffee table. "We'll go later. Where's that book I was reading?"

Jamie was getting just the tiniest bit frustrated. The man wanted to go for a walk, he should go for a walk. The way he was acting, you'd think he was her . . .

Bodyguard.

Jamie sighed, folding her arms across her chest. "I'm perfectly safe here, Chris. You know it as well as I do. There's no need for you to hover over me. As a matter of fact, it makes me crazy."

"I'm not hovering." He pulled the paperback out from under a cushion. "I'm reading. We'll go for a walk later."

It occurred to Jamie that there had been a subtle role reversal here. The neurotic journalist wanted to take a nap. The mellow, laid-back private eye was walking the soles off his sneakers. "Why can't you relax?" she demanded. "Just enjoy doing nothing?"

"Lady, you're talking to the Sultan of Serenity here. I'm perfectly relaxed."

"Really? Then why are you cracking your knuckles again?"

He fixed her with an unblinking stare. "Maybe they needed cracking?"

"I'm trying to make a point here!" Her clear green eyes opened wide and her hands gestured theatrically. "You're constantly checking doors and windows. I have a bruise on my side from hugging you and your damn shoulder holster. The only time you take the thing off is when we . . . well, you know when you take it off. The simple fact is, *no one knows we're here.* I'm perfectly safe whether you hover or not. If you don't ease up a little, you're going to go back to Miami with an ulcer of your own. You don't want to have an ulcer, Marlowe."

"Are you through?" Chris asked mildly.

"Yes." And a fine speech it was, Jamie thought. Clear, precise, and to the point.

"Good. Let's go for a walk."

Jamie flew at him. Her fingers coursed up and down his ribs, tickling him mercilessly. He fell back on the cushions, choking with laughter, trying to capture her wild hands. He was distracted by the wriggling, slipping, sliding pressure of her body against his. She was all over him.

He rolled in a sudden movement, pinning her beneath him on the sofa, holding her hands high above her head. "Say uncle."

Jamie shook her head mutely, her eyes brilliant with delight at the torment she had inflicted.

He looked at her, and the broad smile that curved his lips dropped away by inches. He lowered his forehead slowly to hers, and the laughter faded away as she looked into his eyes. The boyishness and innocence that had sparkled there were replaced with something else.

His hips pressed against hers with a gentle demand. He kissed her softly. "Never mind," he sighed against her lips. "I'll say it. Uncle, uncle, uncle . . ."

Jamie's hands twined into his hair. "Do you still want to go for a walk?" she whispered.

"Yes. In a minute."

Two hours later, they went for a walk.

That night a heavy fog covered the mountains and misted the earth with a fine, soundless rain. Chris built his very first fire without torching a single paper towel, then sat on his haunches tending it with a familiar overprotectiveness. Jamie observed and clapped and nearly got a fireplace poker across her rear end when she rose to her feet and gave him a standing ovation. Giggling, she escaped into the kitchen, feeling cozy and warm and very much in love. She made a nifty little snack tray out of a rusted cookie sheet, filling it with an impressive assortment of junk food. They had potato chips and dip, red and black licorice, doughnuts, cookies, and diet soda.

She carried the tray into the living room and set it on the coffee table. "I think I'm turning into June Cleaver," she said. "Look at this — I've even put fresh flowers on the tray. I must have a hidden streak of domesticity somewhere. How scary."

"I'm surprised at you, Ace." Chris gave up his post in front of the fireplace and headed for the cookies. "Don't you know that in this day and age of the superwoman you can do it all? You can be domestic, ambitious, brave, fragile, aggressive, sensitive, upwardly mobile, and downright sexy. Don't you read Cosmo?"

Jamie opened the bag of licorice with her teeth. "Do you, Marlowe?"

"Nah." He gave her a devilish smile and sank with easy grace to the sofa. "I just look at the pictures. Come sit beside me, sweetheart. I want to grill you."

"I beg your pardon?"

"Grill you. You're always giving me the third degree —"

"For all the good it does me," Jamie muttered.

"— and now it's my turn." He patted the cushion beside him. "Sit. This won't hurt a bit, I promise."

She sat. She crossed her legs, first at the ankle, then at the knee. She uncrossed her legs and folded her hands in her lap.

"This is amazing," Chris said with bright-eyed enthusiasm. "Our Pulitzer Prize baby isn't nearly as comfortable answering questions as she is at asking them."

"Did you want to ask me something?"

"Several somethings."

"Then ask before you get a bowl of clam dip on your head."

"Are all your subjects this cooperative?" He grabbed her hand as she reached for the clam dip. "Don't get mad. I'll be good. We'll start with something easy. What's your favorite color?"

She glared at him. "Well, it isn't pink."

"See? That wasn't so hard." He smiled slowly, a teasing light glittering in his eyes. "We'll move on to something a little more interesting. Why don't you like the idea of being domestic?"

"I'm a journalist." She shrugged,

watching the gentle flames twisting on the hearth logs. "Up until now I've been willing to dedicate all my time and energy to my work. I can't imagine how difficult it would be if I had a family waiting for me at home, wondering why Mommy doesn't have dinner on the table at six o'clock."

There was a short pause. "The career woman's nightmare?" he asked dryly.

"No, not a nightmare." Jamie looked at him, willing him to understand. "Having a family . . . that's a dream for me, just like becoming a writer was a dream. I've just never been able to see a way to do both successfully." She smiled faintly. "I suppose I'm a little fanatical when it comes to dedicating myself completely to my goals. Lessons learned at my mother's knee, maybe. She always told me, if something was worth doing, it was worth doing right. And if I couldn't do it right, I shouldn't try to do it at all."

Chris curved her into his arms, looking down at her indulgently. "Poor baby. How the hell did you ever learn to ride a bike?"

"Fortunately I was a quick learner." She pressed a sloppy kiss on the curve of his jaw. "Are we through with the inquisition? I can think of much nicer ways to pass the —"

"So your mother was a perfectionist,"

Chris said. "What about your father?"

Jamie sighed. "My father was . . . easily frightened. He walked out on my mother three months after I was born. I suppose those two A.M. feedings got the best of him."

"Oh, hell." Chris stared at her, all traces of humor erased from his face. "I'm sorry. I am such a —"

"Lovely, gorgeous, sexy, wonderful man," Jamie finished cheerfully. "Don't swear on my account, Marlowe. I never knew the man. My mother always told me he was terribly charming, but we were much better off without him. I'm pretty sure she was right."

"You're a lovely, gorgeous, sexy, wonderful lady," Chris said softly, hiding the sympathy he knew she would despise. "And I think I'm tired of interrogating you. I would rather ravish your luscious body." He tried to lay her back on the sofa, but there were obnoxious little throw pillows in the way. One by one, they sailed through the air. "I could carry you off to the bedroom," he murmured, "but I don't want to get too far from the food. Do you mind? *Ouch.* Didn't your mother tell you never to hit a man there?"

Jamie grinned, her eyes drowsy with sweet

anticipation. "Mother always said, if something was worth doing —"

"It was worth doing right. I know." Another pillow flew over the back of the couch. "There. Much better, don't you . . . what's this?" Frowning, he held up two crinkled pages torn from Jamie's yellow legal tablet. Jamie recognized them immediately — her notes for the next column on Miselli. Anticipation took a sudden turn toward apprehension.

"I'll take them," she said. "They're nothing, just some notes I made."

If he heard her, he made no sign. He stood up very slowly, his eyes focused on the papers in his hand. "I . . . don't . . . believe . . . this."

Jamie didn't like the expression — or rather the lack of it — in his voice. What a way to ruin a mood. She scrambled to her feet, leaving her heart somewhere in the pit of her stomach. "Look, I told you," she said, trying and failing to sound nonchalant. "I made some notes for my next column. Go ahead and throw them away. I don't need them anymore."

Through his teeth: "Why not?"

Jamie took a deep breath, letting it out slowly. "Because," she said softly, deliberately, "I've already finished the column, all right? Don't stand there like a statue. You must have realized I was going back to work sooner or later."

"Sure, I knew you were going to go back to work." His smile was cold and impersonal and twisted. "I just didn't think you would be stupid enough to go back to Miselli as a topic."

"Who and what I write about in my column is absolutely no business of —"

"When?" he snarled.

"What?"

He crumpled the papers in his fist and chucked them into the fire. "When did you write the damn column? I've been watching you every waking minute."

Jamie stared at him, her fist to her stomach. "You're right," she whispered. "You have been watching me every waking minute. I wrote the column early in the mornings, when you were asleep."

His eyes were brilliant in the flame-colored room. "Hiding from me?"

"I didn't think so," she said flatly, "but looking at you now . . . I suppose that was exactly what I was doing."

"You're going to get yourself killed!" His voice roared in her ears. The emotion in his savage eyes looked very much like hatred. "Is that what you want? Why don't you just

borrow my gun and play a few rounds of Russian roulette? Save us both some time and agony and end it quick. At least then I'd know what to expect!"

"It's a column," Jamie said hoarsely. "It's just a column —"

"It's your damn *life!*" Suddenly his hands were on her shoulders, fingers digging into her skin, shaking her. "Is this all it means to you? Is it? Is this all I mean to you?"

She looked at him through a scalding mist of tears and confusion. She didn't know him, not this man with a world of pain and anger in his eyes. "What's the matter with you? You're hurting me!"

He released her so abruptly, she fell back to the sofa. He stared at her, his skin looking frozen over the hard bones of his face. "Your precious, precious career," he whispered raggedly. "You've got your dream, and come heaven or hell, you're never going to give it up. Congratulations, baby. It's more than I could do." His eyes were blank as he looked at her, through her. "But at least I knew when to let go, Jamie. I knew when to turn my back on my dream and save myself. I wish I could say the same for you."

He left her then, walking out into the night, leaving the front door open and the screen door banging against the frame. Misty rain fell sideways into the room. Jamie watched the hardwood floor grow dark with moisture. It took her the longest time just to gather her thoughts together enough to shut the door. And then she stood in the center of the room, watching the fire die, feeling the cold air seep through the cracks in the walls and around the windows. She had no idea how much time passed before a truth occurred to her, a simple, quiet truth.

He wasn't raging against her demons. He was raging against his own.

She didn't bother with a sweater or jacket. She walked out into the rain, into a darkness that swallowed her. The water ran down her face, beading on her eyelashes, saturating her clothes. The muddy earth dragged at her shoes, and strange noises filled the forest around her. She was sodden, fearful, and determined.

Something moved near the trees. A broad-shouldered figure took shape in the astral darkness, head bowed against the rain. Jamie said his name once, then again, louder. His head turned in her direction, fog swirling like firesmoke around him. Lightning flashed; she saw the diamond-blue glitter of his eyes.

He held out his arms. Jamie ran to him, stumbling over invisible tufts of grass and lumpy boulders before throwing herself into his arms. He held her slender body with all the strength he had, and she felt the muscles trembling in his arms.

"I'm sorry," he said. "Baby, I'm so sorry . . ."

"I know. I know." She clung to him, aching for him, needing him so badly. "You've got to tell me why. You have to tell me what happened to you. I have to understand."

He tipped back his head, letting the rain wash over his face. Still his skin felt hot, so hot. "It's not that easy," he whispered hoarsely.

She held him tighter. "Yes, it is. It's just that easy."

Chris's hands moved up and down her back, the motion awkward and rough. She was probably cold. He should get her back into the cabin, dry her off, fix something hot to drink. He had to take care of her.

He had to tell her. Now.

"She was only four years old," he said, his voice sounding terribly tired even to his own ears. "Her name was Amanda. She was kidnapped from a playground near her house. Every lead we had turned to dust. Finally somebody called in with an anonymous tip, giving us an address. By the time we got there . . . it was too late. It was too damn late."

"It wasn't your fault," Jamie said. The wind took her words away. She doubted he even heard her.

"I had to tell her parents," he went on, his voice growing stronger, focusing. "I'd been carrying around all these pictures of her they'd given me. I took them out of my wallet and gave them back, then I went to the station and turned in my badge. It was as simple as that."

She wanted to weep, but she couldn't. She felt so cold, as if her heart had stopped beating and the blood was chilling in her veins. She took his hand in her stiff, damp fingers. "Come on. We're going back."

The fire had burned down to red coals that glowed brighter when they opened the front door. They undressed in front of the lingering warmth, then went to the bedroom and huddled together beneath the blankets, emotionally and physically spent. Wet hair, cold skin, stiff fingers. It would have been much wiser to have taken a hot shower, but neither of them had the energy.

"Are you all right?" Chris asked quietly.

They were the first words he had spoken since coming back to the cabin.

"Don't worry about me." Jamie's chattering teeth caught the edge of her tongue and she winced. "I'm just fine."

"You're shaking."

"So are you."

"I'm tough." There was a tired smile in his voice.

She kissed his cold cheek. "So am I. Try to remember that, will you?"

"What are you going to do with the column on Miselli?"'

Jamie could hear his heartbeat under her cheek. It had kicked into double time with his last question. "I'm going to send it to Murphy. He'll run it as long as he knows I'm safely stashed away. The fact that I wrote it from my little hideout doesn't hurt, either. It adds an interesting slant. Actually I think it's one of the best things I've ever done. I'd like you to read it."

Chris closed his eyes, grateful for the darkness that hid his expression. "I don't want you to send it in," he said, trying to keep his voice even. He was angry at his own turbulent nature, that after everything they'd been through, he couldn't give her the space she asked for. Quite simply, it was impossible for him. His overriding impulse was to keep her safe. It came first, second, and third. "I don't want you to write about Miselli, I don't want you to think about him. Not yet."

"Then when?" Jamie asked softly. "If not now, when?"

"I don't know. I don't have any answers right now."

Half-formed phrases came and went in Jamie's mind, things she wanted to say but couldn't. Words that might ease his guilt, words that might put his mind at ease. Oh, she had never wished for just the right words quite as hard as she wished now. But they wouldn't come. Sorrow, frustration, and helplessness were all tangled up inside of her, choking her thoughts and leaving her confused and stumbling.

And so she told him what he wanted to hear.

"I won't send the column," she said. "I won't write about Miselli again."

His hands tightened around her. "Please understand," he whispered. "I have to keep you safe. I can't afford to make any mistakes."

Jamie shivered, though not from the cold. "There are all kinds of mistakes."

He tipped up her head to brush his mouth over hers. His body stirred and warmed.

"Does this feel like a mistake?" he asked huskily.

She smiled against his lips. "No."

His fingers spread over her ribcage, slipped upward to cover her breasts. "And this?"

"Umm . . . no." She arched against him, her breathing quietly erratic. "Don't think so . . ."

His hands moved downward to caress her, spreading the growing fever. "Sweet Jamie . . . I've never known anything in my life that felt half so right. When I'm with you, I forget the rest of the world even exists." His lips returned to hers with the most exquisite pressure, molding, coaxing. "Help me to forget, Jamie. Unless you think . . ."

Jamie was working her hands through his hair, meeting him with an open, smoldering passion. "Unless I think . . ."

The movements of his body were hard and hungry against hers. When he spoke, his voice was nothing more than a raw whisper. "Unless you think it would be a mistake? We could always stop."

"Stop?" Jamie's eyes drifted closed, her mind whirling somewhere far away from the tangled web of reality. "Now *that* would be a mistake . . ."

CHAPTER

Nine

"More butter?" Chris asked.

"No, thank you." A short pause. "More juice?"

"No, thanks. I'm fine."

"I could heat up the coffee," Jamie offered.

"That would be nice."

She put the coffeepot on the stove. The cozy little kitchen was filled with the aroma of sizzling bacon. The sun was shining and all the Wyoming birds were gathered outside the cabin tweeting away. Jamie Cross was feeling more claustrophobic by the minute.

What's wrong with this scene? she thought, looking at the man at her breakfast table who was avoiding looking at her. He was shirtless and barefoot, his brown hair soft and fluffy, the morning sun picking out the smile lines at the edges of his mouth. Everything was as it should be. They talked, they ate, they made a stab at identifying the birds swooping past the kitchen window. But they seldom looked each other in the eyes, and when they did, it wasn't for long.

Jamie had never been one for pretense. Last night she had almost managed to convince herself that what they shared was complete in itself, that they had everything they needed to make a sanctuary for themselves in this fragile, unpredictable life. But that's all it had been. Pretending.

She wondered how much time would pass before she could call up the memory of the night before without her heart breaking. He had given her a glimpse of his troubled spirit, helping her to understand. But Jamie knew only too well that sharing his guilt had in no way absolved him from it.

She had promised him to give up her crusade against Jon Miselli. She had lulled his fears into a semblance of quiescence . . . for now. Quietly, sadly, Jamie came to a bittersweet awareness: Last night had ended nothing for him. The guilt and the pain were still there, in the soft shadows of his eyes. How could they build a future together when he was still chained to the past? And when had the stakes become so terribly high?

Chris looked up then, his attention captured by her stillness. "You're awfully quiet all of a sudden," he said, watching her carefully. "What's on your mind?"

You. "How do you want your coffee?"

"Black," he said. "The same way I've had it for the past five days." And then, without warning, without the slightest change in his expression, he dropped a bombshell. "I'm leaving for Miami today."

She dropped the coffee cup. It didn't break, it bounced. Good old plastic, Jamie thought wildly. "What did you say?"

"I have to go back today." He looked at her soberly. "I need to testify at a trial tomorrow morning, something left over from an undercover operation I was involved in. The last thing I want to do is leave you, but I don't have any choice. I'm sorry."

Jamie picked up the coffee cup, her thoughts jumping. "Don't be sorry. You have responsibilities, I understand that."

"I can be back by late tomorrow night," he said. He stood up, flexing the tight muscles in his shoulders and neck. He was tied in knots. He didn't want to leave, but he couldn't stay. Logic told him she was perfectly safe. Logic meant nothing.

"What about your job?" Jamie asked quietly.

"What about it?"

"You've been out of touch for nearly a week," she said. "What about your clients?"

"My clients." He gave a short laugh, as cold and, clear as autumn rain. "They'll survive, believe me. If I'm not around, they'll whip open the old yellow pages and find someone else to do the dirty work. Not to worry."

"But I do worry," Jamie said.

"Look, I told you." He went to her, his hands gently enclosing her face, his fingertips acutely sensitive to the warmth and texture of her skin. "I won't be gone long. As hard as it is to let you out of my sight, I know you're much safer here. I'll be back before you know it."

"You don't understand." She sank against him, and her voice became suddenly tight and soft. "I'm not worried for me. I'm worried for you."

"Nothing's going to happen to me." His smile was whimsical, tugging at her heart. "I'm the tough guy, remember? You're the fragile flower of southern womanhood."

"Not so fragile," Jamie whispered. For just a moment, she allowed herself the luxury of leaning against him, rubbing her cheek over the rich bare skin of his chest. Then she took a deep breath and pushed away, feeling the heartbeats scatter into her throat. "We need to talk."

There was a short pause, thick and strange and uncomfortable. Chris turned his back abruptly, moving to the window.

His eyes narrowed against the slanting light, hiding any nuance of emotion. "So we talk," he said. "This is serious stuff, I suppose? You have that terrifying look of dedication on your face."

"It's serious," Jamie said. Her muscles felt fragile and stiff, as if it would hurt if she happened to move the wrong way. "And terrifying. I want you to stay in Miami, Chris. I don't want you to come back."

His head turned; he looked at her as if she was on the other side of the window, as if he couldn't quite hear her. "What?"

"I don't know how to say this." She wanted to look down, away from those sad-sweet eyes. But she couldn't. "I'm safe here. We both know it. You want to come back and watch over me because of your fears, not mine."

The sound of his harsh breathing measured the unearthly silence. "Is that what you think?" he said finally. "What is this? You believe I'm trying to atone for one failure by taking responsibility for your safety?"

Jamie shook her head helplessly. "Listen to yourself. You use the word *failure*. How did you ever fail, Chris? Did you ever stop caring? Did you ever stop trying? What in the name of heaven did you expect from yourself?"

"Something more than I achieved," he bit out softly. "Don't try to understand, Jamie. You'll never understand."

"You're right." Her voice was as soft and desperate as his. "I don't understand anyone who retreats behind a wall of guilt and self-pity. I don't understand a man with your sense of justice being satisfied with a job that preys on other people's weaknesses. And I don't understand how you can love me when you have so little respect for yourself." There it went, the first tear, dropping off the end of her nose and falling to the floor. "I thought we could make it work, but I was wrong. I could never make you happy, Chris. Not the way I need you to be happy."

He felt like he was dying by inches, but it didn't show on his face. Nothing showed on his face but the biting edge of self-control. "And the love? What about the love?"

She crossed the room, raising her hand to touch the blood-hot skin of his cheek. He flinched, and she drew back. "Don't you see? It's the love I'm trying to save."

His smile was almost frightening. "By saying good-bye?"

"For now," Jamie said. Another tear fell, and another. "But not forever. I need you, Chris. But I need you whole and strong and at peace with yourself. Anything else would be too painful for both of us."

"I see." His skin felt hot and tight, as if it was closing in on him. "Let me see if I've got this straight. In your infinite wisdom and love, you're committing the ultimate sacrifice. You're giving me the freedom to become whatever it is you've decided I should be. If I can manage that, your door will be open. Did I leave anything out?"

She shook back her hair, breathing deeply to keep her voice under control. "Just the truth," she said. "There's no future for us until you make peace with the past. I'll never be able to give you any lasting happiness until you believe you deserve it."

"What the hell do you want from me?" Chris asked softly. His face was hard, and a maelstrom of emotions glittered in his eyes.

"Just a chance." Her voice broke, and she felt the tears stinging again. "I just want a fair chance for us in this crazy world. That's all."

"Someone should have told you." Chris's voice held equal measures of weariness and cool derision. "There's no such thing as fair, Jamie. Not in this life."

She drove him into town. It wasn't a pleasant ride. They spoke little, saying only things that needed to be said. Jamie asked

Chris if he'd remembered to get his sneakers that were on the back porch. Chris reminded Jamie to close the windows at night and to bring in more kindling for the fire before dark. Her tone was hesitant, his was cool. The trip to Clearwater had never seemed so long . . . or so short.

She took him to the gas station in the middle of town, where a rental car was waiting. He got out of the Honda, slinging his gray canvas duffel bag — another purchase from Eldon Don's Variety Store — over his shoulder. A light, sunny breeze teased his hair, creating a soft cloud of color around his face. His eyes were the same fierce blue as the summer sky, though not as warm.

"Don't forget to lock the doors at night," he said.

"Don't worry about me. I'll be fine."

"You'd better be." He dropped a swift, hard kiss on her lips through the open window. "Take care, my love."

And that was that. He turned away without another word and walked into the gas station. Jamie drove back to the cabin, playing the radio at full blast to fill the heavy silence. Cowboy music. It would take a little getting used to, this lone woman in the wilderness role.

Back at the cabin she wandered from room to room, remembering how it was with them. She saw him kneeling before the fireplace, arranging kindling and logs with intense concentration. She saw him standing over the stove in the kitchen, flipping steaks with a pancake turner. She saw him silhouetted against the bedroom window, heard his quiet voice: *Go to sleep, Jamie. Everything's fine.*

She had a headache from the pressure of holding back her tears. She remembered what Chris had told her about going with the flow, about letting nature simply take its course. She smiled and cried at the same time, blubbering until her sobs turned into hiccups and there wasn't a dry tissue in the house.

That night she slept with a pillow in her arms.

Those weren't the last tears she had shed over the next few days, but it was getting better. She had started writing again. She had worked up a series of humorous articles on the life of a fugitive and sent it off to Murphy. She finished her cross-stitch kit through sheer determination. The stitches were uneven and the fabric was spotted with pinpricks of blood, but it wasn't bad for a first effort. She invented a sort of knitting using a crochet hook and made thirteen pot holders. On gloomy days nature and her ulcer demanded a little self-pity. She sat at the window and thought of Chris, and her nose got red and she sniffled a little. On bright, hazy days she picked armfuls of daisies and arranged them in Mason jars all through the cabin. She was surviving. Chris would have been proud.

She was sitting on the front porch making diagrams of a rabbit trap when a familiar Jeep Renegade pulled up in a choking cloud of dust. Casey. Another human being. Her smile felt idiotic, stretching from one ear to the other.

"Morning, Ginger." He was resplendent in an embroidered cowboy shirt with mother-of-pearl buttons. He wore his blinding silver belt buckle and authentic snakeskin boots. His eyes were sparkling in his sun-crinkled face, and the morning breeze cheerfully whipped through his shoulder-length hair. Doctor Fletcher was beginning to look quite normal to her, Jamie thought. Obviously she'd been alone too long.

"Good morning." She patted the porch swing beside her invitingly. "What brings you to my lonely neck of the woods?"

"Can't I come and visit my favorite patient?" He sat down, momentarily distracted by the diagram in her lap. "What's this?"

"I'm designing a trap," Jamie said confidingly. "And then I'm going to build it."

"Are you?" He gave her an amused look. In his very best cowboy twang, he drawled, "Been troubled by bears 'round here lately, ma'am?"

"Rabbits." Jamie's expression was serene. "One in particular. I don't want to kill him, I just want to show him who's boss."

Casey patted her hand in his best bedside manner. "You need to get out more, Ginger. Do something wild and spontaneous. Come into town for a bucket of fried chicken."

"Don't call me Ginger." She looked down at the paper in her lap, feeling the smile grow stale on her face. "Things *have* been pretty quiet around here. Chris had to go back to Miami a few days ago."

"I know."

She glanced up at him in surprise. "You know?"

"Of course, I know. This is Clearwater, remember? He rented a car from Ted Reese at the gas station. Ted's sister Joanne is married to my receptionist's brother, Frank. I not only know that he left town, but I know that he left in a rented mid-size with thirty thousand miles on it."

Jamie stared at him. "You know, this place is kind of scary. If I came into town for a bucket of chicken, would you find out about that, too?"

"Sure I would." He grinned. "Susie Davis works there. She's engaged to my little brother, Clint. She loves to play matchmaker. She'd probably call me up and tell me to get my butt over there while she stalled you. Susie's pretty direct."

"Where you," Jamie replied dryly, "are the soul of tact and discretion."

Casey nodded soberly. "I'm a physician, ma'am. I have a responsibility to the community to maintain a certain dignity. And speaking of responsibility" — he pulled a beige envelope out of his chest pocket — "I have something here for you. It's a telegram. It came this morning."

Jamie's stomach did a quiet little somersault as she reached for the envelope. "You deliver babies and telegrams?"

"Well, not as a rule." He rubbed a hand over his jaw and managed to look a little sheepish. "Believe it or not, my oldest sister's teenage son asked to borrow my Jeep so *he* could deliver the telegram. He works for Western Union in the summer. I very cheerfully offered to deliver it personally.

I'm that kind of guy, you know."

"Scary place," Jamie repeated, opening up the telegram.

It was from Murphy. The message was short and oh-so-sweet.

YOU CAN STOP PLAYING ROBINSON CRUSOE. MISELLI LEFT THE COUNTRY TWO DAYS AGO WITH THE FEDS HOT ON HIS TAIL. FEEL FREE TO COME HOME AND RAISE HELL AGAIN.

"Good news?" Casey inquired, watching her face break out in sunshine.

"The very, very best." She could hardly say the words, she was so wrapped up in her laughter. "I'm going home to raise hell."

"This is important to you?" he asked mildly. "Raising hell?"

"No, not anymore." Impulsively she hugged him, burying her nose in his silky brown hair. "But going home is. Thank you, thank you. Thanks to your sister and your sister's son. I'm going home."

He drew back slightly, his smile faint and almost teasing. "Such enthusiasm does horrible things to my ego, Ginger. Couldn't you act just the tiniest bit reluctant to walk out of my life? Just to make me feel good?"

"I didn't realize you cared," Jamie said in

the same teasing vein. "I'll miss you, Doctor. You have the most unique bedside manner of any physician I've ever met."

"Don't call me doctor." He sighed, brushing a sexless kiss over her cheek. "And you're right about my bedside manner, though it appears you'll never get the chance to see for yourself."

She giggled. "Doctor Fletcher, I'm stunned."

"I'm depressed," he said. "I'm going home to groom Felicia."

Jamie frowned, startled. "Felicia?"

"My horse. An Arabian mare I won at the Days of Forty-Seven Rodeo in Utah. She's devoted to me." He stood up, a suggestion of a grin playing with his lips. "But if *you* should ever decide you can't live without me . . ."

"I'll send a telegram," Jamie promised. She followed him down to the Jeep, her hands pushed deep in the pockets of her jeans, her smile dreamy. She even winked at the pink-eyed rabbit watching them from beneath the porch. "It's a beautiful day," she said happily. "Don't you think it's the most beautiful day?"

He grinned, vaulting into the Jeep. "The most beautiful day, Ginger. Stay happy."

"I intend to," Jamie said.

CHAPTER

Ten

There was a fine art to self-pity. After three solid days of brooding, moping, and sulking, Chris Hogan had it down pat. He didn't eat much. Eating regular meals was a normal and healthy practice. The biting loneliness that surrounded him had no relation to anything as mundane as ordinary mortal processes. He drank too much. He had a permanent hangover, which enhanced his depression with the added dimension of physical suffering. He was truly a miserable human being.

There was no question of sleep. He took to the lonely beaches at night, trudging through ankle-deep water and calling to mind every cherished memory of Life With Jamie. He saw her face, heard her voice, felt her silky-cool hair on his skin. She was with him continually, in his heart and in his mind. He hardly recognized Chris Hogan in this confusing display of vulnerability. The love he felt for her, with her, burned on, undiminished, staggering in its intensity. The accompanying emotions — fear, self-doubt, helplessness — trailed stubbornly behind.

Jamie had entered his soul like a breath of sweet air, bringing to an end the most bitter and empty phase of his life, one he couldn't go back to. Yet, he wasn't quite sure how to go forward. Jamie had given him so many gifts — love and laughter and fresh, bright enthusiasm — but it wasn't within her power to give him peace. That he had to find alone.

There had been a time when he was filled with fear for her. Now he was frightened for himself.

By the fourth day, the very sight of alcohol in any form left him nauseous. He had completely ruined a fifty-dollar pair of tennis shoes sloshing through the surf. And yes, he was suddenly starving to death. He had a good meal and a long nap. He awoke feeling refreshed and slightly hopeful.

He showered and went to his closet in search of an ironed shirt. His casual gumshoe wardrobe was in short supply. The dirty clothes hamper was overflowing with Hawaiian shirts and Bermuda shorts and tacky white socks. The closet was empty, save for the few suits and dress shirts that had comprised his official police detective's wardrobe.

He couldn't really say when or how he finally made the decision. One minute he was staring at the conservative suits and shirts in his closet. The next he was tearing through his dresser drawers, unearthing the last clean T-shirt he owned. He pulled on a pair of jeans that still smelled of woodsmoke. In lieu of his late, great sneakers, his rubber thongs. And then he gathered up his entire police detective wardrobe and carried it out to the Fiat. The shirts were wrinkled, and the suits smelled musty. Unlike crinkled gumshoes, police detectives had a certain dress code to live up to. No shorts, no tacky white socks, no BAD DOG T-shirts. No long hair. No bleary-eyed hangovers.

No painfully empty days chasing cheap, grimy shadows. He was so tired of hurting. It was time to heal.

He took his clothes to the dry cleaner. He got a haircut. He paid a thirty-minute visit to the Monroe County police headquarters. And that evening he took the old Polaroid down to the beach and tossed it into the surf with a triumphant shout. He had no illusions about this uncertain, mysterious world. But for the first time in longer than he could remember, he was ready to accept the fact that he had a place in it.

Right beside Jamie.

Jamie wasn't sure quite what to expect

when she walked into her apartment. Murphy had driven her home from the airport at hair-raising speed, explaining that he was forty-five minutes late to an Associated Press luncheon. Ordinarily this wouldn't bother him. Unfortunately, that afternoon he happened to be the featured speaker, and he suspected his absence would not go unnoticed.

He dropped Jamie and her luggage off at the curb, apologizing through the window while he made an illegal U-turn. He was no gentleman and terribly sorry about it. He'd make it up to her with dinner or a raise or something, someday. Oh, and not to worry, her apartment was livable.

Livable. Laden with shoulder bags and dragging her suitcase up the front steps, Jamie wondered what Murphy would consider livable. The man's office was a health hazard. He enjoyed small furry rodents. His judgment wasn't entirely reliable.

The stairwell smelled of paint. The door to her apartment was propped open with a yardstick, shimmering beneath a fresh coat of enamel. Pearl gray . . . Jamie had always loved that color.

She left her luggage in the hallway, picking her way carefully over the paint-splattered newspapers spread over the floor of the apartment. Someone had cleared away the debris from the explosion. Someone had plastered and painted the living room walls. Someone had replaced the windows and installed a new light fixture in the ceiling.

Someone.

She heard footsteps echoing in the stairwell. Hurried, energetic, purposeful. She turned toward the door, hope tearing through her. And she prayed silently, *Don't let it be Murphy. The disappointment could kill me.*

It wasn't Murphy. Chris filled the doorway, his features frozen in an expression of surprise. Eyes wide. Jaw slack. A stripe of pearl-gray paint on his cheek. Several more stripes and smears on his BAD DOG T-shirt. Chris.

"You're home," he said.

Two words. Hardly an intimate greeting, yet his husky voice went through her with flickering heat. Jamie felt an honest-to-goodness, soul-deep smile taking over her lips and her eyes and her heart. "I'm home," she whispered.

"You look good," he said. He had to concentrate on maintaining his emotional poise. It wasn't easy. He'd dreamed of it happening just like this — walking through the door and finding her waiting for him. Seeing her smile. Hearing her voice. Having a dream come true unexpectedly tended to throw a cynical soul into confusion. "I was hoping to have the apartment ready before you got back."

"*You're* responsible for all this?"

His expression was guarded. "You saw the crack in the kitchen wall, didn't you? I can explain. This was kind of a learn-as-you-go proposition for me. The damn plaster dried so fast, I barely had —"

"I haven't seen the kitchen yet," Jamie said. Her eyes felt itchy from the fresh paint and tears held back. "And no one has ever done anything like this for me before. I don't know how to thank you."

He shook his head, holding her gaze. "There's no need. You know that."

Silence fell between them, heavy and demanding. Jamie struggled to find the right words to disguise the urgent needs and quiet excitement that twisted her muscles into knots. If she moved too quickly or in the wrong direction, she was afraid she would snap like a piece of brittle taffy.

For the first time she noticed he was carrying a gallon of paint in each hand. "I didn't mean to keep you standing there," she said breathlessly. "Come in. Let me take the paint. Where would you —"

"Jamie." He put the paint down. His expression was friendly and sustaining, and she would never have guessed what it cost him to keep it that way. "This is me, remember? I've been making myself at home here for the past few days. You don't need to play the hostess routine. Just relax."

"I'm relaxed." She took a shaky breath and steadied herself. What a shame her sofa had been blown up. She wasn't sure how long her traitorous knees would hold her. "I'm just a little . . ."

His expression took on the faintest hint of amusement. He came to her, his hands dropping lightly on her shoulders. Gently he said, "You're just a little . . ."

"Stunned," she whispered. "And so very, *very* happy to see you, Marlowe." She nestled against him with a sigh, cradling his waist in her arms. Heart against heart, they stood silently, gradually adjusting to this new reality. They were together, and simply holding each other brought pleasure to them.

"Hi," Jamie whispered against his throat.

He smiled into her hair. "Hi."

"Wyoming was empty without you."

"Miami's been a wasteland. I drank too much. I couldn't sleep. I ruined my Reeboks."

Jamie tipped back her head, her lips curving in a hazy smile. "Your Reeboks? How did you —"

"Never mind." He gazed down at her, the backs of his fingers touching the heat in her cheeks. "I could stay like this forever. Holding you, just holding you . . ." He bent his head, the brief pressure of his lips over hers exquisitely gentle, almost reverent. His smile was shaky. "You could break my heart, Jamie Cross."

"And you could break mine." Her lips tipped in a one-sided grin, her fingers walking over his shirt buttons one at a time. "Go ahead, Marlowe. I'm putting my heart in your hands. Do with it what you will. You've painted my living room and kitchen and bedroom. I think I can trust you."

"Actually, the bedroom isn't painted yet. I just finished patching the Sheetrock this morning. But I guarantee that . . . Jamie?" The expression on his face suddenly flashed from dreamy to dismayed. "You haven't seen the bedroom yet?"

"Well no, but —"

"Then wait here." He released her so quickly she almost fell. "Hell, I should have known something like this would happen. I'll be right back. Why don't you bring in your luggage from the hall? I'll just . . . take care of something in the bedroom. It's no big deal, really. Just . . . wait here."

He should have known better, Jamie thought, watching him practically sprint from the room. She was a reporter. She had an overabundance of healthy curiosity. And heaven and Chris Hogan knew she didn't take orders well. Surely he didn't expect her to do as she was told?

She followed him into the bedroom. He was prying the lid off a gallon of primer with a pocket knife. She couldn't imagine what had suddenly inspired him to paint . . . until she saw the brand-new mural he had created on the bedroom wall.

There was a heart. A slightly lopsided, pearl-gray heart. And within the heart was a bold, boyish declaration: *Christopher loves Jamie.*

She whispered, "Oh, my goodness."

Chris jumped. "I knew it. You couldn't give me five minutes to cover it up, could you?"

"Why would you want to cover it up?" There was a tremor in her voice. She crossed the room, staring at the heart with moist green eyes. "I'm glad you didn't.

"I was just fooling around," Chris said woodenly. His face was flaming. "Testing the primer. I love you, you know I love you,

but . . . I'm a mature adult, for Pete's sake."
He cleared his throat. "I didn't think you'd
see it before I painted over it."

"Did I ever tell you what I was like when I
was growing up?" Jamie asked softly, still
staring at the heart. "You should have seen
me, Marlowe. My hair looked like a fluorescent Brillo pad. I was a tomboy. I refused to
wear anything but jeans and high-top
sneakers. In short, not the kind of girl whose
initials were carved in the old oak tree." She
turned then, smiling at him through a veil of
tears. "The mural stays."

"It's no mural." Chris shoved the pocket
knife back in his jeans. "This is so damned
embarrassing."

"Don't be embarrassed." She stared at
him, lost in the clear blue of his eyes. Tenderness flowed through her, hot, sweet,
achingly familiar. "Something's changed in
you," she said quietly. "Something's different. I can't put my finger on it, but . . .
you seem happier."

"You're here," he said simply.

She shook her head. "No, it's more than
that. It's that you're not . . . angry inside . . .
the way you used to be. I could sense it
before, that anger — even when you were
laughing, even when you were giving your
lectures about relaxing and going with the

flow. And now . . ."

He had become quite still. "And now?"

"I don't know." Her smile was faint, her voice husky. "Maybe you've taken your own advice. And maybe I'm just crazy."

"Not crazy," he said. He crossed the short space between them, taking her hands, holding them tightly. "Somehow you managed to know me better than I knew myself. It wasn't an easy thing to accept. I did a lot of soul-searching when I came home, Jamie. And I discovered you were right." A crooked grin here. "Don't look so astonished. I'm capable of recognizing the truth, even if it takes me a little longer than most men."

Jamie's breath caught. "The truth?"

"I was burying myself in guilt. I wanted to be Supercop and save the world, but I discovered I was only human. I had a few hard lessons to learn. I could bleed, I could cry, I could hesitate. Sometimes I could win, but sometimes . . ." He swallowed hard, and just for a moment the shadows were back in his eyes. "Sometimes I could lose. That lesson nearly killed me, Jamie. No, don't say anything, let me finish. After I came home I realized —"

"Hey, partner! You painted yourself into a corner yet?"

A third voice, Jamie thought stupidly. A woman's voice. She looked at Chris. "There's a stranger in my living room," she said. "A strange woman."

"Not so strange," Chris sighed. He looked over his shoulder, then back at Jamie, his gaze whimsical. "In any case, you'll meet her yourself soon enough." Then, louder: "In here, Carolee. Watch the walls, they're still wet."

"I've already discovered that." A tall blonde with a Prince Valiant haircut sailed into the room, holding up two painted palms. "You couldn't have put up a sign or something? Am I supposed to be psychic? Well, hello there." This to Jamie. "What a pleasure to finally meet you. You must be Jamie. I recognize you from Chris's enraptured descriptions."

Carolee? Partner? Enraptured descriptions? Jamie was speechless. She looked at Chris, her eyes pleading for mercy.

"Jamie Cross, I'd like you to meet Carolee Greene." Chris paused, holding Jamie's eyes. "My new partner," he said.

It took her a moment to put two and two together. Her eyes opened wide. She whispered, "You went back. You're a . . . what are you now? Officer Hogan?"

"Detective Hogan, Monroe County Precinct. Very little pay, very long hours." He looked at her, and deep within the clear blue eyes was a light of contentment and wonder. "And do you know something, Ace? It's a good feeling."

"It's been lovely meeting you," Carolee said brightly, "and I can understand why Chris was stupefied. Now I will wait downstairs in the car like the sensitive individual that I am. Don't be too long, Chris. We're due at the station in fifteen minutes. My goodness, what romantic graffiti. You should be an artist, Detective Hogan."

Carolee left them with a wave of her paint-smeared hand. Jamie waved back, but her eyes were blank. She was still adjusting. "She seems nice," she said huskily.

"She is. She also doesn't mind doing the paperwork. We get along just fine."

"Well . . . good."

"My car's in the shop. Carolee's been running a taxi service."

Tonelessly, "That's nice of her."

"She's also married."

"Oh." A *very* nice woman, Jamie decided.

"Two kids."

"Oh."

He was looking at her in the old way, part heat and part amusement. "We need to talk, Jamie. There are so many things . . ."

"I know." His eyes were bright, hungry, promising pleasure and hinting at dreams. She gazed into them wistfully for a moment, then said softly, "But you have to go."

"I have to go." He raised his hand, tracing his finger slowly around the curves of her mouth. So soft . . . "Have I told you I adore you?" He grinned when Jamie pointed at the wall. "Yeah. Well . . . you'll have to forgive me. I'm an absolute beginner when it comes to mad, passionate love. Now and then my impulses get the best of me."

"You're forgiven," Jamie said. "And adored back."

"I'd better go." Reluctance was in his voice and his eyes. "Newly reinstated police detectives can't afford to be late."

"Your clothes . . . ?"

"I can change at the station. Listen, I've got a couple of deliveries coming here this afternoon. Are you going to be home?"

"I'm too tired to go anywhere." She heard a car honking. She stepped back, tearing her gaze free from his. "You should go."

"I'll call."

She glanced around the room. "Do I have a phone?"

"Not yet, but you will." He walked backward to the door, keeping her in his sight. "I've taken care of everything, Ace. Just lay your weary head down and sleep away that nasty old jet lag."

"No bed," Jamie said sadly —

"When will you learn to trust me?" His smile was tender and not quite innocent — the smile she could never get away from in her mind. "I told you, I've taken care of everything. I'll call you. I love you. Don't back up, you'll stick to the wall."

She smiled mistily. "What am I going to do with you?"

His smile stretched. "The possibilities are endless."

At three o'clock that afternoon, a rainbow was delivered to her apartment.

Jamie stared at the John Denver lookalike who stood in the hallway with a huge cardboard box. "What do you mean, you have a rainbow for me?"

"That's what the man ordered," John said. "A rainbow for your living room. It's a skylight, lady. Stained glass and one of my best works, if I do say so myself. Are you gonna cry?"

"Forgive me," Jamie said, sniffling. "I'm an absolute beginner when it comes to being adored. Come in."

At four o'clock the friendly installer from the phone company arrived. At four-fifteen

Madsen Furniture Company delivered the most beautiful brass bed Jamie had ever seen in her life, complete with silk sheets and a down comforter. At five-thirty Jamie picked up a paintbrush and added another heart to her bedroom wall: *Jamie loves Christopher.*

She slept like a baby that night, stirring only once when the telephone rang.

"I'm sorry," Chris said. "I woke you."

"What time is it?"

"Midnight. I just got off duty."

"Thank you for my rainbow. And my bed."

"You're welcome. Go back to sleep, baby."

"Come over."

There was a long silence, then a sigh. "No. You're tired. Besides, I have a couple of things I need to take care of first thing in the morning. I'll pick you up tomorrow at noon."

"That's nice." A yawn. "Are we going somewhere together?"

"Yes, sleepy love. We're going somewhere together."

He picked her up in a newly waxed Fiat that fairly purred. The windshield was repaired, and both door handles worked beautifully.

"Nothing's too good for you," Chris said solemnly, opening Jamie's door.

"I'm touched," Jamie said. "You know, this is the perfect car for a police detective. Not too flashy, not too conservative."

"It's a good thing I changed professions," Chris said. "Buckle up, sweetheart. We're going for a ride. And stop flicking my hula dancers."

They drove west, following a quiet, two-lane highway through green pastureland — and into a misty wall of cypress stands. This was Florida's wilderness, and although Jamie had been born and raised here, she had never seen this unspoiled beauty. It reminded her of Wyoming, though it was softer, more gentle. The air was rich and heavy, leaving a fragrant sparkle on her skin and eyelashes. Snowy egrets, serene and majestic, dotted the wire fence that followed the lip of the everglades. Jamie was stunned by the lushness of the scenery. She couldn't believe she was only an hour's drive from the heart of the city.

They traveled on a paved highway, then a gravel road, then a short, winding path that was crowded with vegetation. Jamie blinked, then suddenly a cabin appeared in the dense sawgrass. It wasn't as large as the cabin in Wyoming, but it looked sturdy and well-kept. The front porch was screened off from the mosquitoes with a heavy steel mesh. The copper roof gleamed dully in the hazy light.

"What's this?" Jamie asked curiously. "It looks like a southern version of Capwell's Homestead."

"That's exactly what I thought the first time I saw it. Come inside."

"Do you have a key?"

"Silly child. Didn't I tell you I would take care of everything? Come."

He had a key. They toured the entire cabin, which consisted of one all-purpose room and a bathroom. Chris pointed out the nice overstuffed couch, the nice rocking chair, the fine mattress on the fine box spring. He also made a fuss over the circular rock fireplace that rose from the center of the cabin.

"You hate damn fireplaces," Jamie said, automatically using his Wyoming vocabulary.

"I don't hate damn fireplaces anymore," he said. "As a matter of fact, I fancy myself a master fire builder now."

"Do you?" He was up to something. It was in his eyes and in his sweet, little-boy smile. "I hope I don't seem vulgarly inquisitive, but . . . what are we doing here?"

217

"We belong here." He sat down in the rocking chair with an extremely satisfied sigh. "It's ours."

"Ours? Our what?"

"Our cabin."

Jamie closed her eyes briefly, then tried again. "You're telling me this cabin is ours? Yours and mine?"

"Your name's on the deed." His smile grew. His eyes sparkled blue laughter. "Along with mine. So I guess it's ours. Would you like to sit down?"

"I think I'd better." Jamie started for the sofa.

"No, not there." He patted his lap. "Here."

She sat on his lap, nestling against him. His mouth wove a teasing pattern up and down her neck. Jamie held on to his shoulders, brushing her cheek against his hair in an affectionate and sexy gesture. "So are you going to explain?" she asked huskily.

He kissed her soft, soft mouth. "Now?"

Against his lips — "Now."

"Fine." He sighed, leaning his head against the chair back. His hand moved absently through her hair. "I missed the peace and quiet of our Wyoming hideaway. And my house doesn't have a fireplace. I don't want to lose my talent for laying fires. What did you say?"

Jamie's eyes were unusually bright. "Nothing."

"Fine. A friend of mine told me about this place. I bought it two days ago. My cash flow has dwindled to a trickle, but what the heck? This is a treacherous and uncertain world, my love. We need a place to run away to now and then. A sanctuary. I can practice my fire building, and you can take potshots at rabbits. We'll be very happy here."

Jamie laid two fingers against the pulse in his throat, feeling it jump beneath her gentle touch. "I don't like it," she said.

"The cabin?"

"No." Her hand floated down the open neck of his shirt, caressing the smooth brown skin, her eyes shining with pleasure. "Between us, we have two homes and one cabin. I think that's terribly extravagant."

He flashed a brilliant, breathtaking smile. "My thoughts exactly. I still have to paint your bedroom, you know. It could take me months, years even."

"You'd better come live with me, then," Jamie murmured, her face taking on a sweetly drowsy expression. "For months, maybe even years."

"Whose name would come first on the mailbox?"

"We'd have to work that out."

"It would probably be easier if we had the same name."

"Probably." Jamie was desperate to abandon herself to his touch, to the growing need deep within her body. But first . . . "I need to ask you something."

"Yes, I'll marry you."

"Thank you." Holding his face in unsteady fingers, she whispered, "Now I want to ask you something else. Did you go back to police work because of me?"

"Yes and no." His eyes were alive with sparks of contentment and certainty. "It was my decision. But you're the one who taught me never to give up on a dream. Any more questions?"

"One." Her eyes hungrily touched on every part of him. The tousled, honey-colored hair. The feverish blue eyes. The tiny little scar on the cleft in his chin. She was aching for him, wanting and needing him so badly. "Where do we go from here?"

"Sweet, sweet Jamie." He pulled her closer, his voice thick and rich with the quality of a man speaking to his lover. "The possibilities are endless."